# TEAMMATES

## The Quarterback and His Son

### PART V

# Kevin Davis

# Table of Contents

"I'm not a fan of soccer, I'm not interested in it. But if you're going to be on a team, make sure you wear comfortable pants."

~ John Cleese

## CHAPTER 1

# DAVE: LOCKER ROOM

I sat on the bench attempting to pull off my socks. I ached all over. It had been a good match. My legs were caked in mud, which had solidified in my leg hair. I wiggled my toes, enjoying the feeling of being able to stretch them out as the sweat evaporated from them.

"Good game!" Todd said, standing across from me. I looked up to find him standing at his locker in just his jockstrap, his smooth, pert ass accentuated by the blue straps.

"Yeah! Good match," I said, pulling my jersey over my head. I stood and smacked his butt so that a light print of my hand appeared, outlined on his ass. He thought nothing of it, smacks on the ass were commonplace in the locker room especially when we won and were celebrating.

"That goal you scored in the second half was amazing," Todd said. He was referring to the complete fluke of a goal I scored when he passed the ball to me, and I managed to get it past their goalie. The truth was, I'd kicked it wrong. I'd not intended to kick it where it ended up going. Maybe that was enough that the goalie got confused and went left instead of right.

"Thanks for the assist," I said, stepping out of my shorts.

"Anytime," he said. The way he said anytime seemed to hint at something more than the game. I dismissed it as purely my imagination. Todd was straight and had a girlfriend. I'd met her. She was one of the hottest girls on campus. Todd was hot in his own right, tall, light to medium build. Light blond hair covered his arms, but his chest was smooth and hairless. His bright pink nipples stood out against his pale skin. He was clean-shaven except for the fuzzy blond caterpillar that sat below his nose. I wasn't sure whether the mustache suited him but it was a popular facial accessory among a certain demographic online. His long blond hair was pulled back and tied up into a man bun. With pouty lips and bright blue eyes, he was definitely popular among the college girls. He seemed oblivious to all but Daniella. He worshiped her, maybe to his detriment. She treated him like a worm, which just made him want her more.

I pulled down my jock and let my thick, soft cock dangle in the cool air. Sweat evaporated from it and my balls as I tugged them mindlessly. I caught Todd glancing down quickly, then looking away.

He pulled down his jock, bending forward slightly to get it down his legs. His bright pink pucker came into view. It was hairless and smooth like most of him. His balls hung down between his legs in a tight, clean-shaven sack. He stood upright again, hiding his hole in the curve of his smooth ass. It could have easily been a woman's ass if you took away the balls, so round and plump with a nice bump out. I'd never really considered myself an ass man until recently. Brian had changed that. His ass, like Todd's, was larger and fuller than most guys. It had that thickness that made you want to fuck it, which I did often. I'm sure he'd be waiting for me back in the room, naked and dripping in anticipation for my return still musky despite the shower I was about to take.

I still couldn't believe everything that had happened over Homecoming weekend. It seemed like a dream that I was just now waking up from. I tried not to dwell on it especially now, but I couldn't help think of Uncle Jim and Brian's dad. All that time I'd lived with Jim I never imagined something like that would happen but now it had and I was still processing it.

Todd turned, and I saw his dick, plump and pink with a tight foreskin. It sat atop his balls and jutted straight out in defiance of gravity. His pubes were shaven completely like his balls. He'd told me once how much Daniella liked them that way. And whatever Daniella liked, he did like the obedient lapdog he was.

"You should really shave yours. It feels so good," he'd said running a hand over the smooth sack.

"Nah, I like my wild jungle," I'd told him. It would be too much hassle, and Brian liked it this way. He went nuts for my hairy body, licking my chest and funky pits.

"See you in there," Todd said, turning to grab his towel and heading toward the shower. Raucous laughter exploded every once in a while from the shower room that was filled with at least 9 guys at the moment.

I grabbed my towel and followed Todd's pert ass as it shifted with each step. If I wasn't careful, I might pop a boner watching those mesmerizing cheeks bounce. His back was also smooth and lean, with just the right amount of muscle rounding out his shoulders and lower back.

Steam hit me as I stepped into the shower room. It was large and rectangular with nozzles at regular intervals around the perimeter.

"Good game," Matty said, grasping my shoulder as I headed into the cloud of steam. All around me was naked flesh, some hairy, some smooth, all wet. I'd been okay being in a room full of naked guys before, but something in the way Todd looked at me set me on edge. I could feel my dick rising, and I had little control over it.

"Looks like Meat is happy to see me!" Matty laughed smacking my ass. They nicknamed me "Meat" because of my dick, which looked bigger than anyone else's on the team, even when it wasn't hard.

"Bend over, and I'll show you a good time!" I replied, smacking his ass. He waved it seductively at me, smacking it a few times before breaking out in a roar of laughter. The other guys joined in. It was always a good time when we won a match and celebrated together in the locker room. It was all just good fun; nothing was actually meant by it. Sure, there was that strange mix of homoeroticism and homophobia, but they were good lads for the most part.

Todd took the shower in the corner next to me. I thought I caught him looking down at my meat again. I let him look as I lathered up my chest and let the suds drip down my body.

"You two need a moment alone?" came Matty again. I looked down and realized Todd was also hard.

"We'd better get out of here quick, looks like it's catching!" He called out. Todd gave an embarrassed look and turned toward the wall.

"Thinking about Daniela's big, beautiful ass, I'm sure!" I said, covering for him. I'd have to see if maybe there was something more to his looking than just curiosity.

The banter went back and forth as we finished showering and we headed back to our lockers. By then, my dick had controlled itself and merely swung heavily from side to side as I headed to my locker. Todd stayed in the shower long after everyone else left.

"Rubbing one out in there," Matty called out to Todd. Matty could be a bit much and didn't know when to stop. He was a big guy, hairy from head to toe with a tight-cut dick that seemed to get lost in his wild pubes. His balls were enormous though, pulled back close to his body in a tight, leathery, dark sack. He was not ashamed to walk around the locker room naked, and so I'd seen his bare ass a great deal since joining the team. While others started out being rather shy about nudity, he was not and set the example making it okay for others to join in. Now it seemed wrong not to be naked after a game or practice.

Todd came out quickly, grabbing a towel and headed to his locker. It wasn't like him to hide his body with a towel like that. What had gotten into him? I wondered.

I started to get dressed, letting him take furtive glances down at my softening dick.

"You wanna grab something to eat with me?" I asked.

"Um, sure," he said, snapping his eyes back up to my face. He blushed at being caught looking.

I stood naked, messaging Brian. I knew Todd was using the opportunity to check me out again.

"Mind if we swing by my room first?" I asked.

"Sure," he said, following me out and across campus.

I tried messaging Brian again, but my messages went unread. I wondered what he was up to.

I should have knocked when we got to my room, but I wasn't thinking. I just put my key in and pushed the door open. Todd gasped, and I looked up to find Brian standing naked behind that hairy guy from down the hall, the one we'd seen at the gay campground.

He was on his back getting pounded by Brian's thick cock. They both looked over in shock when they saw us in the doorway.

## CHAPTER 2

# JUNIOR: CONFIDANT

"I hope everything is okay?" Ravi asked the day after my dad had visited.

"Yeah, it's all good," I said.

"That's a relief," he said.

"Why do you say that?" I asked.

"Your dad seemed worried when he stopped in looking for you and Dave," he said.

"Oh," I said.

"Now that I've met him, I'm jealous as hell that you got to see him naked," Ravi said. "He is one seriously hot daddy!"

"Ugh, that's my dad you're talking about," I said, though I secretly agreed with him one hundred percent. If he only knew what we'd done. Who knows, maybe he'd think it was hot. I wasn't about to tell him, though. It was bad enough Dave knew, he'd kill me if anyone else ever found out. Especially the fact that he'd fucked his uncle!

"Sorry man, I can see where you get it from. Is he as hung as you?", he asked.

"I don't know. Why would you ask me that?" I said, trying to look disgusted by the idea or at least indifferent. I'm not sure if I succeeded in either.

"I didn't see you come in last night, where did you guys go?" Ravi asked.

"We went out for dinner with my dad and Dave's uncle. It was late, and we'd been drinking, so we stayed over at Jim's rental," I said.

"Nice!" he said, giving me a look like he knew something more had happened than just sleeping over. I looked around, trying not to telegraph my excitement on my face or body. My dick jumped, thinking back on Jim's hairy body and thick cock. I couldn't help it.

"Something happened, didn't it?!" Ravi said, giving me a mischievous grin.

"No!" I tried to lie, but somehow Ravi always knew when I wasn't telling him the truth.

"You got it on with Dave's uncle, didn't you?" he said.

"I'm not saying we did, but lets say we did, would that freak you out?" I asked.

"Not at all. My cousin and I fooled around all the time. It's no big deal," Ravi said.

"Really?" I asked. I was taken aback at his nonchalant attitude.

"Sure, traditionally in my culture it's not incest for even first cousins to do it. Plus, though it's not discussed much, many relatives like brothers and uncles will have sex. Since women are fairly segregated from men outside of marriage, a lot of stuff goes on between men. It's just not talked about, but it's pretty common," Ravi said.

"I always thought they were kinda homophobic," I said.

"Oh yeah. It is a contradiction. If someone comes out as gay, it is a huge deal. It could get you killed in some places. That's the paradox of it all. It's like, have all the gay sex you want in the closet, but don't you dare talk about it or identify as gay or bi," he said.

"That's nuts," I said.

"You have the same things here. How many of the most vocal bigots turned out to have a secret gay life?" Ravi said.

"True enough," I said thoughtfully. My dad had been one of them, though he'd changed a lot since the camping trip.

"So was this encounter with Dave's uncle really hypothetical, and does it have anything to do with your dad showing up here in a panic looking for you?" Ravi asked.

He put the proverbial two and two together and made four. It didn't seem like as big a deal to him. I thought I may as well come clean with him.

"Well, kinda. It's a little complicated," I said, shifting around trying to find a way to say what I wanted to say.

"There is more to that camping trip than you let on, isn't there?" Ravi said.

Once again, I was dumbfounded at his perception. Was it somehow written on my forehead that I'd slept with my dad? He didn't need me to answer. He could read my reaction.

"Fuck! You really did! Now I'm even more jealous!" Ravi said laughing. He was taking it better than I ever would have expected.

"Yeah, after I caught him with Collin, things started to happen," I said.

"Did he fuck you?" Ravi said getting straight to the point. I blushed bright red.

"Oh shit!" He said. His dick was poking up in his bright yellow shorts. It was clear he was turned on by the idea.

I nodded. The cat was out of the bag.

"What was it like?" He asked. "Does he have as big a dick as you? Did it hurt?"

"Wow, slow down," I said. Clearly, he was interested in all the gory details. "Yes, his dick is just as big as mine, maybe bigger. We didn't actually measure or anything," I said. "And yes, it did hurt, a lot actually, but Colin helped open me up and teach me how to take a big dick."

"Fuck! I wish they were still here!" He said, rubbing the material where a wet stain was forming.

"It's your own fault for going up to New York. How was that, by the way?" I asked.

"It was a blast. We saw a Broadway show, went to Times Square, saw the Statue of Liberty, all the tourist spots," He said.

"How's your sister doing?" I asked. That was the main reason he went to visit. She was going to be there before heading up into Canada.

"She's good. She said to say hi to Dave from her," he said. "I didn't have the heart to tell her he was already taken," he said with a wink.

"I know he liked her," I said. It was hard not to have a twinge of jealousy. Dave and I had been with a few guys now, including my dad and his uncle, but for some reason, I didn't feel threatened by them. Ravi's sister, on the other hand, made me nervous. It wasn't like that was ever going to happen, but it did remind me that Dave was still questioning. Would he ever want to explore the other side of his bisexuality? Would I be as okay with that as I was with him playing around with Darrel?  I tried to shunt those thoughts away. It was unlike me to be jealous. It was just that I loved Dave so much I couldn't help but be a little possessive.

"She seemed to like him too," Ravi said. He studied my face for a minute. "Don't worry, it's not like that. She's got a boyfriend already."

A wave of relief washed over me. I realized I was tensing my jaw and relaxed.

"Yeah, I met him in New York. Really great guy. Fucking hot too. Part of why she wanted to visit the US. Our parents don't know. I'm sure they wouldn't approve," He said.

"Oh, why?" I asked.

"He's Jewish," he said flatly.

"Oh, I can see how that could be problematic," I said. There had been protests on our campus, but not like those going on around the country. The tension was still palpable.

"That's putting it mildly," he said, miming his head exploding.

"Speaking of exploding heads, I'm contemplating telling my mom I'm gay. My dad already knows, of course. And now that Dave is out to his uncle, it seems like it's time I told her and my sister," I said.

"I don't know. Didn't you tell me she's a bit of a religious nut?" he said.

"Yeah, but maybe knowing her son is gay will change her mind," I said.

"Or she kicks you out of the house, and they stop paying for school," he said. "My family would, at the very least, disown me if they knew."

I hadn't thought about what it would mean if things did go badly, would Dad cut me off? Most of my way was paid through loans, grants and a small scholarship. If it came to that I would be ok, I'd just need to maybe get a job to make up the difference or take on even more debt.

"I hadn't thought of that. I just hate not sharing what Dave really means to me. When we talk on the phone, I always have to be careful about what I say," I said.

"I know it's tough, but I'd think seriously about what it would mean. It's not something you can take back," he said.

"I know. That's why I'm stressing," I said.

"You've got time. Think it over," he said. "In the meantime ..." he continued rubbing his dick through his shorts. "You made me so horny talking about your dad earlier."

"Too bad I don't have a picture of him naked for you," I said.

"Fuck! I would kill to see that," Ravi said. I couldn't believe he was so into my dad.

"Give me a minute," I said, grabbing my phone. I wrote a text and waited. A few minutes later, the screen lit up.

"Here you go!" I said, holding up my phone with the image of my dad's massive cock filling the screen.

"He actually sent you his dick pic?" Ravi asked, grabbing the phone and his cock.

"No, I asked Colin if he had one," I said.

"Oh, damn," Ravi said, clicking play on a video that just came up in the chat.

There was my dad with a huge ebony cock slipping between his lips.

"Fuck! I never knew about this one," I said, watching with delight as my dad expertly sucked that big mechanic's cock.

"Fuck! I wish I'd known. Maybe I could have seduced him," Ravi said.

"Knowing what I know now, I believe you might have been successful," I said. I imagined my dad's dick sinking into Ravi's furry brown ring as I pulled my dick out and stroked it.

Ravi smiled and leaned forward to take it in his mouth.

"Your dick looks just like his," he said, holding it by the base and comparing it to the photo. I blushed. Colin had said the same thing.

"I would love to see you take his dick," I said.

"I'd love to have the two of you take turns fucking me," he said, turning over and pulling apart his cheeks to reveal his hairy hole. It looked glossy and ready to take me. I jumped up and pressed my head into it.

"Fuck!" He cried out as I forced my way in.

"You want this dick, don't you," I said, mimicking my dad's voice.

"Fuck yeah, sir," Ravi said, instinctively going along with my role-play.

"My son has told me all about you. He says you have a really nice ass," I said, trying not to giggle at how ridiculous I sounded.

"I love to take his big cock. Now it's your turn to breed me, sir," he said.

I enjoyed imagining I was my dad. I imagined what it would be like to be him. I stood a little taller and pushed out my chest, enjoying his confident stance. I was always a little shy about my body, unlike him. He'd always been in pretty good shape, beginning when he was young and into sports, long before I was born.

At least I knew now my dick rivaled his own. It gave me confidence knowing I had a well-above-average cock. Ravi moaned as I flexed my cock, stretching his hole. I thought about Dave fucking my dad, then his uncle, and found I was already unloading inside of Ravi.

"Oh fuck!" I roared.

"Yeah, breed my hole, daddy," Ravi said, stroking himself so vigorously that the whole bed shook.

"Fuck!" He yelled. I felt his hole clench down on me and release multiple times as he ruined his bed spread. I pulled out and flopped down next to him as he collapsed on his bed, as a stream of my cum seeped out of his used hole.

"That was so fucking hot!" He said.

"It was," I said, catching my breath and rolling onto my side so I could run my hand over his smooth, tan skin.

"Can you send me those?" He said, nodding at my phone.

"Sure, just don't share them!" I said. I imagined him looking at them as he jacked off and fingered his ass for years to come.

"They will remain in my secret stash, I promise," he said, crossing his heart.

## CHAPTER 3

# JUNIOR: GIRLFRIEND TROUBLE

"She seems nice and all, but I thought you liked guys?" I said to Ravi on our way back to the dorm after dinner a few nights later. Dave was at a game, so I'd met Ravi and his new girlfriend, Amani.

"I still do. You do understand what bisexual means, right?" Ravi said.

"Of course, but I just never pictured you with a girl," I said.

"I've dated girls before. I find I'm much more romantically connected to women. When it comes to guys, it's all about the physical, but with women, it's more emotional. If that makes any sense," he said as we reached the hall.

"I guess so," I said, trying to keep an open mind. I realized I could be just as bigoted about my own perspective as others were towards me.

"I mean, it's not going to stop me from sucking your dick every chance I get. Speaking of which, you want to come in for a minute?" he continued, nodding toward his room down the hall.

"Sure," I said, knowing where this was headed. As soon as we were inside, he reached down and tugged at my shorts. Before I could react, he already had my soft, but rapidly growing, cock in his mouth.

"And she's okay with this arrangement?" I asked.

"I haven't told her yet," he said between sucking my shaft and licking my balls.

"You might want to before it gets too serious," I said.

"I know, it's just I really like her, and it's all so new still," Ravi said, sitting back and pulling off his shirt. His cock poked at his jeans as if it would rip through the denim. He unzipped his fly, and the underwear-clad member popped out of the opening. There was already a wet spot forming on the light blue fabric of his briefs.

"I get that, but it would be infinitely better to tell her than her to find out on her own," I said. It wasn't like our trysts had gone completely unnoticed, despite Ravi's precautions.

Ravi turned around, facing away from me, and tugged down his jeans and underwear, revealing his big hairy brown ass. He reached back and pulled his cheeks apart and winked his hole at me, impatiently waiting for my tongue or dick to satisfy him.

"I know, I know. I'm just waiting for the right time. It's not like I can just say, 'nice evening, I hope it's not going to rain. I really like getting my ass railed by my hallmate's fat 8-inch cock,'" he said as if the invitation wasn't already very clear. I skipped rimming him out. He was too impatient for the main event for that. I grabbed his bottle of lube and squirted some on his ass and my cock. I slicked it up, then ran my finger down the hairy strip running down his crack until I found his hole. It was smooth and silky feeling to the touch. Two fingers slipped into it easily. Between my visits and Darrell's, who was also stretching his hole regularly, he'd learned to love taking a big cock.

For some reason, Dave had never wanted to fuck Ravi. In fact, Dave seemed to only want to fuck me, apart from that one time with my dad and his uncle. I'd fucked him on occasion, but it was becoming more and more rare. I think he enjoyed fucking me more than getting fucked, which I didn't mind. He's an amazing lover, and I absolutely love his big, cut cock. The fact that we have an open relationship and I could fuck Ravi on the side balanced things. I worried though, that Dave seemed to not take advantage of the fact that our relationship was open. It made me feel just a little guilty when I was in the mood to top.

Ravi waited patiently for me to line up my cock with his hairy hole. I squirted some lube on my cock and pressed three lubed fingers into his hole. It felt good to feel around inside him like this. The image of Colin's fist slipping into Timmy's stretched hole filled my mind. I wondered what it would feel like to stretch a hole out like that. I pulled out my three fingers, poured more lube on them, then pressed all four fingers and my thumb into a point. I pushed in, feeling his tight hole resist my advance. My dick became increasingly hard as I pushed forward, watching more and more of my hand disappearing into Ravi's light brown hole.

"Whatever you are doing, don't stop. That feels amazing," Ravi said, leaning his head back, his eyes rolling back until I could only see the whites of his eyes.

I was up to my knuckles inside him when I hit a wall.

"Fuck! I feel like I have you and Darrel inside me at the same time," Ravi said.

"Close," I said, pulling my hand out and illustrating what had been inside him with my left hand wrapped around my knuckles of my right hand.

"You had your fist that far in?" He asked.

"Yup," I said.

"Wow, I didn't think that was possible," he said.

"I saw a friend of mine take a fist past the wrist up his ass," I said.

"Fuck!" Ravi said.

"I also saw him take two dicks at once," I said.

"That would be so hot! I've watched some women doing double penetration in porn before," he said.

"I've wanted to try it since seeing Colin and my dad fuck Timmy," I said.

"This happened when you went camping with them?" He asked.

"Yeah, we met this guy, Keith, who let us stay with him while Dad's car was in the shop. Timmy was the tow truck driver," I said.

"Damn! That sounds amazing!" He said.

"Yeah, it was. I'm so glad you're cool with all this. I've been dying to tell someone," I said.

"Like I said before, that is the hottest thing I've ever heard. My sex life is pitiful compared to your escapades," he said.

"Colin and I took turns fucking Timmy later that evening. He had so many loads in his ass after that night that he was leaking all around my cock," I said.

"Crazy to think your dad's cum was among them," he said. My dick jumped at the memory of fucking Timmy and feeling Dad's load lubricating him. I leaned forward and pressed my cock into Ravi's hole, feeling how loose he was. I fucked him, letting my mind wander back to that night in the hot tub and the morning after when Dad had finally fucked me.

I pumped my worked-up load into Ravi's hole, grunting and moaning as I imagined it was my dad below me taking my cum. I leaned in, slipping out of Ravi's hole as I went down on him. I pressed two fingers into his wet hole while I sucked his cock. I could feel my load oozing around my fingers. I found the hard lump and jabbed at it.

"Oh fuck," Ravi grunted as he clamped down on my fingers, squeezing them together and expelling some of my load onto the bed. My mouth filled with his cum, warm and salty.

I swallowed and cleaned him up, reaching for a towel to clean the cum off my fingers and dick.

Ravi's phone buzzed, and he grabbed it.

"Oh shit, she's on her way up," he said, scrambling to get up.

I looked around for my clothes scattered around.

"No time," he said, tossing me the towel I'd used to clean up my cum. I grabbed the bundle of my clothes and wrapped the towel around my waist as I darted into the corridor.

"Hey!" he said as I barreled into someone short, rotund, and hairy, in my haste to leave.

# CHAPTER 4

# JUNIOR: HALL MATE

"Oh, sorry," I said, stepping back from Adam as he bent down to pick up his dropped shower kit.

He stood and handed me my shorts, which had also fallen when we collided.

I heard the door to the stairs creak open behind us and remembered why I was in a rush to leave Ravi's room.

She spotted us just outside his door. I felt my towel slipping and tried desperately to keep it in place.

"Hello again," she said, giving me an awkward smile.

"Hi," I said, blushing uncontrollably.

"Ravi in?" she asked.

"I ... I ..." I started but was at a loss for words.

"Yes, I saw him heading back from the bathroom a few minutes ago," Adam said.

"Oh," she said, knocking on his door. Adam took my arm to lead me away.

"Just a sec," came a call from inside Ravi's room.

As we turned the corner, I spotted a disheveled Ravi open the door. His eyes swept the corridor, spotting me and Adam. He gave me a scared look.

"Hey, I was wondering if you wanted to go to ..." was all I heard before we headed into the bathroom.

I turned to look at Adam as he set down his shower kit, took off his towel, and hung it by the shower opening.

"Thanks," I said, smiling at him weakly. I'd been meaning to hang out with him after running into him at camp, but it never seemed to happen. I'd gotten lost in classes and Dave. I knew I'd been neglecting my friends.

"That was Ravi's girlfriend, I take it ?" He asked.

"Uh, yeah?" I said.

"And I take it she doesn't know about the two of you," he said.

"Uh," I didn't realize our trysts were common knowledge.

"I saw you go into his room earlier," he said with a knowing, awkward smile. He was usually pretty shy, and we didn't say much to each other. We'd pass each other in the hall, and I'd say hi, and he'd say hi and give me a look, and that would be it. He'd caught me in some very compromising situations in the past.

"Yeah, he's bisexual, but she doesn't know," I said.

"It's cool, I won't say anything," he said, stepping into the shower area. He must shower at odd times because I'd not seen him in here in a while. I wondered if he felt weird about showering in the open room with the other guys. He was heavy-set and covered in hair from head to toe. He was by far the hairiest guy I'd ever seen, and I'd seen quite a few.

I followed his wide, hairy ass as he took up a position at the farthest shower nozzle. I dropped my clothes on the bench and hung up Ravi's towel. I could still taste his cum in my mouth. I laughed as I thought at least he didn't have to clean up a bunch of cum from his chest since I'd taken care of that.

"Sorry about ..." I said, not really sure what I was sorry about. I felt guilty for not getting together with him and Chris at the camp. He looked at me with a questioning expression.

"I mean, I'm sorry we didn't get together at the camp," I said.

"Oh, that's okay. The festivities were rained out, sadly," he said, facing away from me and lathering up his front.

"I know, that was a hell of a storm," I said.

"I went back last weekend. It was closing weekend," he said.

"Oh, too bad I didn't get a chance to go again. I really enjoyed it," I said.

"I was a little too cold to be naked, but at least the hot-tub was nice," he said.

"I bet it was hopping," I said.

"Yes, I was," he said.

"How's Chris?" I asked.

"He's doing fine," he said. It was difficult to carry on a conversation with him. I regretted not being more friendly sooner.

"Can I borrow some soap?" I asked.

"Sure," he said, turning a little to the side to hand it to me but still keeping his front facing away. I took the bottle and lathered up my chest and armpits, then focused on cleaning off my cum-slicked cock. It wasn't hard but wasn't exactly soft either. It was in that post-orgasmic state where it still looks impressive but hangs down instead of up against my abs like when it's fully hard.

I caught Adam looking down at it. He looked away quickly. I could see his face reddening.

"Relax, it's okay," I said, giving it a few strokes for his benefit. He looked down and followed my hand movements, is mouth opened slightly.

He looked around nervously but didn't move, keeping his eyes fixed on my dick. I was getting hard again. I looked down at his wet body. The hair was matted where it ran down his back and over his ass and into his ass crack. His ass looked inviting.

"You have a nice ass," I complemented him. He blushed and looked away.

"You have a nice dick," he said, nodding at my now hard cock. I hadn't seen his dick yet, so I couldn't comment. It was like he was afraid to turn in my direction.

"You are welcome to touch it," I said. He looked around shyly then reached out his hand. I stepped closer and looked down. I could now see what he was hiding. He was holding his hand in front of his crotch. I recalled that first time in the shower when he went past. His dick was hidden amongst his thick bush. This time it was hard and stuck up from his bush, barely three inches long and not very thick. He looked down at it, embarrassed to be seen.

I dropped to my knees in front of him and took all of it in my mouth, rolling my tongue around it. I buried my nose in his wet pubes. It was nice to not be gagging on an extra large dick like Dave or Darrel's for once. He whimpered as I ran my tongue around his sensitive head. I was fascinated by it. He was leaking profusely, and I could taste its sweet saltiness.

He grabbed my head and tried to pry me away. I heard the door close and pushed myself back, remembering we were in the open shower and could be overseen.

"Oh, sorry, I'm interrupting," Ravi said, looking in from the shower entrance. Adam turned to face the wall, not wanting Ravi to see his tiny dick wet with my spit and leaking a steady stream of precum.

"It's okay, Adam and I were just getting reacquainted," I said, smiling. I was glad it was Ravi that caught us and not one of the other guys on our hall, who may have been more inclined to report us.

"Thanks for the save back there," he said to Adam, who nodded shyly.

"Yeah, that was close," I said, turning to Ravi so he could see my fully hard cock pressing into my abs. He laughed at the sight of it, shaking his head.

"Never enough, huh?" He said.

"You know I'm always horny," I told him. It was true. I had to get off a couple of times a day, or I'd never be able to focus on my studies.

"I'll let you get back to it. I'm heading to the fine arts building. Amani asked me to go to some play this evening. She's downstairs waiting," he said.

"Well, don't keep her waiting," I said, stroking my cock enticingly. He looked down and licked his lips. I knew he wanted to suck it. It came as a shock when I felt lips clamp down around it. Adam grew bold and swallowed me to the hilt while Ravi watched in astonishment.

"Fuck!" He said, grabbing his shorts front as he watched Adam go to town on me.

"Shouldn't you get going? She's waiting," I said.

"Oh yeah, right," he said, still planted where he stood. His dick was obviously hard under his hand. He looked down at it, poking out the front of his pants. If he wasn't careful, he might start to develop an unsightly stain on the front of them.

"Fuck!" He said again, tugging them down to let his hard cock out for air. I stroked Adam's hair as he gave me one of the best blow jobs I'd ever experienced. He was really good at it. I loved fucking and was usually not that into blow jobs, but his mouth was better than anything. He rubbed my shaft with his slicked-up hand as he licked around my head. I grunted my approval, looking down at this hairy beast devouring my cock.

"He's really good," I said, pulling back as I was getting close already. "Show him," I commanded, not sure where the authority in my voice came from. He obeyed without question and knelt down in front of Ravi.

"Oh fuck!" Ravi cried as Adam slipped his cock into his mouth.

"I know, right!" I said. Why had I waited so long to get with Adam? I could picture the look on Dave's face when Adam took his big cock deep in his mouth. I'd have to make that happen sometime.

It seemed like in no time Ravi was spraying his cum down Adam's throat. He'd only just given me his load less than 30 minutes ago. I knew the feeling. I was ready to cum again watching Adam slurp up Ravi's cum, not missing a drop.

"Damn, now I have to change again," he said, looking at the water splashed on the leg of his pants.

"Oh, sorry," Adam said, backing away.

"It's okay. Totally worth it," he said, smiling as Adam stood and joined me again.

"Have fun tonight," I said as Ravi turned to head to the door.

"That was unexpected," I said, smiling.

"You both have nice dicks," he said, reaching down to grab mine again.

"You too," I said, tugging at his with two fingers.

"Nah, I know mine is nothing," he said, looking too embarrassed to accept a compliment. I honestly didn't care about his size. His hairy body and incredibly skilled mouth more than made up for it. Sure, I loved a big dick stretching my hole, but I doubted he would be fucking me anyway.

"You want to come back to my room? My roommate is away this weekend," he said.

"OK, we could go to mine, as long as you don't mind Dave potentially coming back and joining us," I said with a wink.

"Oh, okay," he said, beaming. I recalled the way he looked at Dave when we were in the pool together. Most people had that reaction to Dave. Maybe I'd get to see that face sooner than I thought.

We got out and dried off, then headed across the hall to my room.

"Sorry about the mess," I said. I wished I could blame it on Dave, but I was a bit of a slob too, so it just compounded.

"It's okay, my roommate is a pig," he said. I could see now why I didn't see much of him in the hall. I got the sense from his tone and comment that he didn't like his roommate very much.

I pushed Adam back onto my bed and pulled off his towel, letting mine fall into a pile at his feet. I sank back onto his cock, marveling at how easily it fit in my mouth. He sat back, whimpering as my tongue swept over his sensitive underside. I tried to give him as good a blow job as he'd given me, but I knew I didn't have near his skill. I licked down his shaft to his balls, which were pulled in tight against his body. They were completely covered in thick black hair; the hair even went up his shaft on either side, sprouting out in thick waves.

His dick pressed into the mat of hair up and to the left. Precum leaked out of his wide piss slit and formed a line, getting lost in his bush. His head was wider than his shaft, with a prominent ridge. I licked around the ridge and savored the precum.

He grabbed hold of my head and pushed me down as his legs came up. Below his balls, his taint was as lost in hair as his hole. I licked down from his balls as he guided my head to his hidden crevasse.

I tasted it more than saw it. Hair flossed my teeth as I licked his hole. He moaned in pure delight as my tongue twisted up his passage. He was much more open, and his hole deeper between his fat cheeks than I'd ever known anyone to be.

He jammed my face into his hole with such force that I thought he might break my nose. I held my tongue rigid and fucked his hole with it until it ached from overexertion.

I sat back and brought my cock up next to his. The difference was striking. I could eclipse his completely when I pushed it down over his. He laughed.

"See, mine gets completely lost next to yours," he said. It was like he welcomed the comparison. Like he wanted me to humiliate him with the comparison. I felt bad doing it.

"Yeah, but it felt nice in my mouth," I said, trying to help his self-esteem.

"I don't mind, I know I'm tiny compared to yours," he said, smacking his dick hard like he was scolding it. "I really love a big dick," he said, swatting at my cock so it bounced up and down against my belly.

"You don't mind being called small?" I asked.

"Long ago I accepted what nature gave me. Now I kinda get a kick out of being put to shame by a huge dick like yours," he said.

"So you don't mind if I say something like, my pinky is bigger than you?" I said cringing as I said it. Far from being offended, he brightened and his dick jumped.

"Yes, tell me how superior your dick is compared to mine," he said. He was leaking a steady stream of precum all over his mushroom head and down his shaft.

"At least 10 of your dicks could fit inside my big cock!" I said.

He rolled his legs up to his chest, exposing his wide, hairy ass.

"I bet one of those could easily fit inside this!" He said, nodding toward my dick while slapping his ass.

I took the hint and got under him, teasing his hole with my dick. I let it slip up against his balls.

"Smack my balls and dick hard as you want," he said.

I smacked my cock into him again. He winced in pain but nodded to do it again. I cupped my hand and smacked his balls harder than I intended. My balls pulled up inside me in sympathy.

"Fuck! Do that again!" He cried. I couldn't believe he actually got off on it, but his little dick was dribbling precum all over his hairy belly.

Smack! Echoed around the room when my hand came down harder on his balls. I winced in pain along with him.

"Now wreck my hole! No lube, just jam that big fucker in there!" He said, pulling both ass cheeks apart to show off his wet hole.

"You want this dick!" I said, batting his battered balls with it.

"Yes, please, use my pussy!" He said. I never liked referring to my ass as a pussy, something too feminizing about it for my taste. But in this case, I made an exception. His was a beautiful, hairy pussy. Without warning, I shoved my cock in his tight hole. It burned going in dry. His eyes shot open, and he let out a loud grunt. I ignored the pain and didn't stop until my pubes rested against his ass.

"Fuck!" He cried, gritting his teeth, his eyes open wide. I didn't wait for him to adjust to my girth. I plowed in and started fucking him intensely. A steady stream of expletives escaped his lips, but he didn't try to stop me. If anything, he nodded reassuringly while at the same time he slammed his fists down on the bed.

His ass felt amazing, loose but also hugging like a thick blanket, if that makes any sense. His wide ass jiggled as I pounded it. I reached down and slapped him hard, so that my handprint appeared bright red against his white skin.

"Yes, hurt me!" Adam screamed, pushing up and grinding his ass against my pelvis. I was deep as I could go.

As I fucked him hard, I felt my balls slapping into his skin with each thrust. He was whimpering, his dick creating a pool of wet, sticky hair on his belly.

"Breed my hole!" Adam said, sweat pouring down his face.

I continued to fuck him, feeling like I was getting close but having a hard time finishing. It could have been the fact that I'd just cum in Ravi's ass not too long ago. I felt Adam tighten his ass again, and more precum dribbled out into his hairy belly. His eyes rolled back, and his body shook. His dick jumped multiple times as he clamped down on my cock.

I was too lost in Adam's ass to notice when the door clicked open.

"Oh shit!" came an unfamiliar voice.

"Oh, sorry about that. I'll come back later," Dave said, letting the door shut as I caught sight of Dave's teammate looking down at Adam with my cock still lodged in his ass.

## CHAPTER 5

# DAVE: THE TRUTH

"Oh shit!" Todd said.

"Oh, sorry about that. I'll come back later," I said, letting the door shut.

"I didn't know your roommate was gay," Todd said, backing away from the door.

"Yeah, he's supposed to put a sock on the door when he has company," I said. It had been the rule initially, but ever since we started fucking, that rule had fallen by the wayside.

"You're okay with having him as a roommate," Todd asked.

"Yeah, he's cool," I said. I wanted to tell him he was more than just my roommate. I wanted to go in there and join him in railing Adam. I had no reason to stay in the closet now, but still, I hesitated.

"Guess we'll let them finish and just head over to grab some dinner," I said, as I turned to go back toward the stairs.

"Okay," Todd said, still looking at the door as if he could see through it.

"He ever ... you know," he asked.

"What?" I said.

"You know, has he ever tried to do anything with you?" Todd asked. I looked at him, trying to decide if I would outright lie or come out to him now. He did seem to be checking me out in the locker room, so maybe he was a bit curious himself. I hesitated. I had to say something.

"He did, didn't he!" Todd said, seeming to read it on my face. I felt the blood rush to my face as I blushed from ear to ear.

"Don't tell anyone else on the team, okay?" I said. I wasn't ready to be out to the rest of the guys.

"You actually let him?" Todd asked. It was then I realized he's just been asking if he'd ever propositioned me. Not if we'd actually done it. I felt like an idiot.

"Yeah, I figured why not see what it was like. I figure I'm bisexual," I said. Though by now I felt like I was beyond bisexual and definitely closer to full on gay, but maybe saying I was bisexual would be more acceptable to Todd.

"Wow, I would never have pegged you as doing anything like that," Todd said.

"Don't knock it. There's something about being with a guy that's incredibly hot. It's so different than with a girl," I said. I couldn't believe I was telling him that. He looked at me and then back at the door as if longing to open it again and get another look.

"You ever consider doing it?" I asked point-blank.

"Nah, it's not for me," he said, puffing up his macho exterior, but the outline of his dick in his shorts told a different story.

"You sure? I saw you checking me out in the shower," I said, taking a risk he might get defensive.

"Who doesn't look at your dick, Meat," he said, using my nickname.

"I know most of the guys look, nothing wrong with that," I said.

"Just jealous, I guess," he said.

"Especially Matty," I said.

"He's always parading that tiny dick of his around the locker room," he said, with a laugh that seemed to break the tension between us.

"It takes all kinds," I said.

"Wow, so like what do you ... I mean ..." Todd started and stopped.

"You really want to know?" I asked. I wasn't sure what I would tell him. Todd blushed.

"Just can't believe it, that's all," he said.

"You won't tell anyone, will you?" I asked.

"I won't say anything," Todd said.

"Okay..." I said, trying to think where to start, when the door opened and out came Adam, looking a little sheepish. He spotted us and quickly darted down the corridor.

"Hey, sorry about that," Brian said, looking at me then Todd with a curious eye. He seemed to know when to play along. "I forgot to put the sock on the door."

"It's okay," I said, giving him a wink that Todd wouldn't notice. "Have you met Todd?"

"No, other than seeing him at the games," he said, holding out his hand. Todd looked at the hand as if considering whether it was safe to touch or not.

"Nice to ... ah ... meet you," Todd stammered. His eyes focused on Brian's softening dick, clearly visible in his tight shorts. He noticed the state of Todd's cock pressing against his thigh and lifted an eyebrow. I shook my head no.

"Sorry I missed the game, did you win?" Brian asked, changing the subject to my relief.

"Yes, Meat ... I mean Dave here scored the winning goal," he said. Brian looked at me with a wide grin. I don't think he knew about my locker room nickname, but he seemed to approve of both.

"That's awesome!" he said.

"I was going to drop my kit off and see if you wanted to join us for dinner?" I asked.

"I ate with Ravi and his girlfriend earlier," he said.

"Oh, Ravi has a girlfriend?" I said, looking surprised. I remembered that first night on campus when Brian sucked his dick right in front of me. It shocked the hell out of me at the time.

I'd had a complicated relationship with sex all my life. I won't go into what I talk to my therapist about, but it took a lot to separate what was done to me by my dad in Africa and what happened with Brian. I was so confused at the time. I still am. I never would have thought I'd fall for a guy, not in a million years, but there was something about Brian. The way he was so understanding. I'd never told a soul about what happened to me until I told him.

Something opened up in me that weekend I can't explain. A part of me I'd run from for so long I suddenly confronted. I didn't have to fear it anymore. I embraced it. Fear and shame had no hold on me anymore.

"Alright, guess Todd and I would grab something then. See you later," I said, dropping my bag inside the door and heading back into the hallway.

"Okay, see you later," he said. Todd looked back once more before following me to the stairs and back over to the cafeteria. Unfortunately, it was already too late for dinner service by then, so we grabbed some food at the 24-hour mart on campus and took it over to the quad. It was unseasonably warm for late October, so we sat on top of a picnic table and ate.

"I can't believe you guys did it," Todd said, coming back to the subject again unprompted. Something was going on there beyond simple curiosity. I saw the way he looked at Brian's dick in his shorts. I was actually surprised he bothered to put on clothes. He rarely did around the room anymore. Not that I minded. His nudism was part of what pulled me out of the closet. I'd watch him parading around the room in nothing, seeing his dick bounce around, and I felt myself getting aroused.

Once I got the courage to join him, I knew it was inevitable. I wanted him more each day I saw him, but I was afraid of that desire in me. He helped me let go.

"Okay, ask what you want to ask?" I said.

"Huh?" Todd said.

"I know you want to know more, so just ask," I said.

"Oh, uh," he stammered.

"Maybe you want to know what exactly we've done?" I said. He squirmed uncomfortably.

"Did he suck your dick?" He asked. I nodded.

"What was it like?" He asked quietly.

"Fucking amazing. He really knows how to suck dick," I said.

"Fuck. Daniella was great at it, but she never gives me head anymore, barely lets me fuck her," he said.

"I find gay guys are almost always up to at least suck your dick, and they know their way around them too. I guess it helps to have one," I said. Todd looked up at me like he was going to say something but stopped himself.

"You want to know if I ever did it," I asked, anticipating what his question might have been.

"Did you?" He looked at me incredulously. I nodded.

"Fuck!" He said.

"It wasn't as bad as I thought it would be," I said.

"I think I'll pass," Todd said, scrunching up his nose at the idea.

"I'd give you one if you wanted," I said, wishing I could take back the words before they reached his ears.

"Really?" Todd said.

I rested my hand on his thigh. He looked down at my hand, just inches from the head of his dick snaking down his shorts. It was throbbing hard, pushing up the material of the thin shorts. If there hadn't been people wandering around, even this late, I would have pulled down his shorts and blown him right there.

I felt him tense up at the touch. I pulled my hand away, feeling like I'd misread this situation. What was I doing? Was I trying to recruit Todd for him? Like I'd done for my dad ... I stopped myself. I was visibly shaking.

I thought back on what I'd done for my father back in Africa. It was bad enough what he did to me, but I'd become his accomplice, bringing others to him. I felt so ashamed now.

I gripped the table tightly and pushed the intruding thoughts away, taking a deep cleansing breath like my therapist told me to do when I got overwhelmed.

"I'd better go," I said, standing up.

"Is something wrong?" Todd asked, of my abrupt shift in mood.

"No, just ..." I left it at that and grabbed my trash, tossing it in the bin nearby before rushing away. My heart was racing. What the fuck was going on with me?

## CHAPTER 6

# JUNIOR: SURPRISE VISITOR

"Shit!" I said as the door closed and I saw Dave disappear from view. I was so distracted I didn't realize he was cumming again until I felt his ass tighten around my cock. I looked down to find his little dick spirting massive ropes of cum all over his belly. It was more cum than I'd ever seen anyone produce and it wasn't showing any sign of stopping. His hair was thick with great globs of the stuff. He grunted and his legs spasmed as he shot another load. I'd lost count at this point. With each one his ass tightened around me, milking my cock.

"Holy fuck!" I said as I started to cum inside him. A geyser of milky white seed spurted from his piss slit. Was he still cumming or was he cumming hands-free for a second time? It got me thinking. Maybe this was evolution compensation for a small penis. A big dick can penetrate deeper and deposit the little swimmers closer to their target. To compensate, a smaller dick scatters shots massive amounts of the little swimmers in hopes that one will make it. Only one needs to anyway.

I thought about my poor swimmers inside of Adam now, lost in his colon, no hope of reaching a viable target. I almost felt bad for them. Then again, it's not like a tissue or a toilet paper or a shower stall wall was that much better. At least an ass was warm.

Finally, Adam's cock stopped pulsing and spitting and fell limp into his deep, wet bush. The cum was everywhere. It dripped down his balls and leaked onto my sheets. It spilled over the side of his wide belly like drizzled icing running down the sides of a cake. I bent down and licked some off him, which elicited a giggle as he pushed me away. It was watery and salty with a hint of sweetness.

"I'd better go see about Dave and his friend," I said, handing Adam a towel to mop up the great puddle of sperm. He got dressed and headed out, looking back at me awkwardly.

"I hope we can do that again soon," he said.

"I hope so too," I said with a wink. He rounded the door just as I pulled up my shorts. Dave and his friend were still in the hall.

"Hey, sorry about that. I know I should have put the sock on the door," I said, covering for Dave in front of his teammate.

"It's okay," Dave said, introducing me to Todd.

"I was going to drop my kit off and see if you wanted to join us for dinner?" Dave asked.

"I already ate with Ravi and his girlfriend," I said.

"Ravi has a girlfriend?" Dave looked a little shocked.

"Yeah, he's been keeping her a secret from us, but it seems serious," I said. Dave shook his head.

"You can leave your gear here if you want. Pick it up later," Dave offered.

Todd looked at me, then down at the lump of my dick pressed into my shorts. He looked horrified but also curious. I'd have to talk to Dave later and find out if he felt the same vibe from Todd as I did.

They left their backpacks by the door inside the room and headed out for dinner.

I felt uneasy about the whole thing. I could tell Todd was checking us both out. He was interested in something. The question was, did he know it or not?

I went back in and laid back on the bed, feeling some damp patches of Adam's cum under me.

I woke later and checked the time. It was after 2 a.m. and Dave had not returned from dinner. I had to admit Todd was a hot jock, and given the opportunity, I would have hit that, no question. I was surprised Dave would go off like that without at least letting me know he wouldn't be back. I checked my phone. No messages other than the ones he'd sent me while I'd been fucking Adam.

Was he mad at me for that? He knew I fucked around with other people. It wasn't like that was a secret. We had an open relationship, as far as I knew. We hadn't really talked about it, but given all we'd done together, it seemed to be a given.

He was so hard to read sometimes. I knew he was going through some rough shit in therapy. I'd found him on his bed one afternoon when I came back from class, curled in a ball, weeping uncontrollably. When I came in, he pretended like he hadn't been. He kept things bottled up inside him so much. I worried about it.

"You okay?" I wrote and waited to see if he read it. I saw the three dots appear then disappear a moment later. He'd sometimes get into these moods. I understood. I just hoped it didn't have anything to do with me.

"Want some company?" I said, sitting up in bed. I was awake now and wouldn't be getting back to sleep for a while anyway.

Again, three dots appeared then disappeared without a reply. I got dressed and checked the temperature. I slipped on a hoodie and grabbed Dave's hoodie from the chair. It was Friday night, so even though it was 2 a.m. there were still students milling around campus, some getting dropped off after a night at off-campus bars and clubs.

I knew where I'd find him at this time of night. If it had been the daytime, I'd know he probably took a hike.

I climbed the spiraling staircase until I reached the top. The door was propped open with a brick. I stepped out, careful not to let it close behind me. I walked around to the far side of the roof until I spotted the figure in a tight ball, legs pulled up to his chest, shivering slightly. I placed the hoodie over his shoulders and sat down next to him.

I didn't say anything, just held his hand and put my arm around him. By the dim light, I could see the wetness on his cheeks. We sat in silence for minutes that stretched on. He leaned against me, sighing.

"It's okay," I said, hugging him close, "I'm sorry about earlier and your teammate seeing that."

"He knows," he said.

"Oh, shit, sorry," I said.

"It's okay, I doubt he'll tell anyone," he said.

"What happened?" I asked.

"He was asking about you and if we ever did anything. I didn't want to lie, so I told him," he said.

"How'd he react?" I asked.

"He seemed curious," he said.

"Oh, did anything happen after that?" I asked.

"I put my hand on his leg, but then I kind of freaked out and left him sitting there," he said.

"Oh," I said.

"He probably thinks I'm a freak or something," he said.

"I doubt it," I said, trying to reassure him. He'd told me about the guys on the team and how he wasn't sure they'd be very accepting if he came out to them. I'd been pleasantly surprised by how open people had been with me. By now, I think most people already knew I was gay. The only person that didn't yet was probably my mom.

I could understand his conflict. There is something about being on a team, the camaraderie between straight guys. Would they act the same around him?

I held him tight and just comforted him. I knew what he was going through couldn't be easy.

## CHAPTER 7

# DAVE: ROLE PLAYERS

I woke up with Brian holding me, his naked body pressed against mine. I sighed, knowing I'd soon have to get up and go meet the team for an away game. We had a long drive ahead of us, and we'd be staying there tonight before coming back tomorrow morning. I dreaded seeing Todd. What would I say to him?

I wanted to just stay here in bed with Brian all day and never leave. I felt him stir, and his morning wood poked me in the middle of my back. I was also hard and needed to piss, but I also craved him inside me. Most of the time, I just wanted to fuck him, but sometimes when I'm feeling vulnerable like today, I give  myself over to him.

 I pushed back against him, pressing his hard cock between my ass cheeks. It felt so big and thick, rubbing along the hair on my ass. He gave a soft moan in my ear and pulled me close, reaching lower to find my dick.

"Morning," he said softly in my ear.

"Morning," I said, stretching and pushing back against him, rubbing his cock against my ass again.

"You okay?" He asked. In response, I pushed up so he slid down, and his cock head rested in the cleft of my ass, just above my hole.

"You sure?" He asked. I nodded. It had been a few weeks since he'd fucked me last. I had to be in the right mood, but sometimes even when I was, I'd back out at the last minute. Something would trigger a memory, and I'd tense up. I tried to do what my therapist suggested and take a break and a deep breath. Brian was more than understanding. I knew he got frustrated with me at times, but he tried not to show it. That's why I was cool with him fucking other guys. I didn't want to disappoint him; he was so good to me.

Today I was ready; today it was just him and no ghosts looking over my shoulder. I wanted him, no, needed him inside me. The thing with Todd had me riled up. I wanted him, but had I misread that he wanted me too? I remembered what his hard dick looked like, and as Brian pushed into me, I had a vision of Todd's dick pushing in. I wanted to be present here with Brian, but I couldn't escape the feeling that I wanted it from him too.

"Mmm, fuck me, Todd," I said without thinking. Brian stopped for a moment, his dick planted firmly inside me. I tensed up, realizing what I'd said. Then he bent low, and I felt his body press into mine.

"Yeah, you want your bro's dick, don't you," he whispered in my ear.

"Yeah, give it to me bro," I gasped as he nearly pulled out then rammed into me hard.

"Yeah, I bet all the boys on the team would love a crack at this ass and cock," he said, reaching below me to tug on my hard cock. I pushed up to give him access and was now on all fours with my ass in the air. I imagined I was on a bench in the locker room as the team lined up around us, stroking their meat, waiting for their turn. I gave into the fantasy and pictured each of them naked as each one dumped a load into my stretched hole.

"Oh shit!" I cried as my balls tightened and my ass clenched. Rope after rope of cum sprayed the bed below me. Brian stepped up the pace and slammed into me again and again until I felt him pulse inside me.

"Fuck yeah, bro, breed my hole," I gasped as he filled me with his load. I collapsed forward onto my steaming cum, while keeping Brian inside me. He pressed his chest to my back and held me, warm and safe in his arms.

My alarm buzzed in the background, but I let it go on as we held each other close, and I felt his cock soften inside my sore ring.

"Fuck that was hot," Brian finally said as he pulled out and mashed the snooze button on my phone.

I felt his cum dribble down onto my balls. I couldn't believe the amount of cum he still had, knowing he'd just fucked Adam the night before and probably Ravi before that if I knew him.

"You must really be into Todd," he said.

"I don't know," I said.

"It's okay if you are. He's super hot. I'd fuck him," he said.

"I doubt that is going to happen. I think I misread him," I said.

"Really? I get that vibe from him. I think he's a little more than curious," he said.

"So you think he's curious too?" I asked.

"There is only one way to find out," he said.

"I don't know if I should risk it," I said.

"Give it time. I will bet you anything he'll make a move," he said.

"We'll see," I said as he rolled off of me. I laid there in that puddle of wet cum, not wanting to move.

Smack! My ass bounced as his hand struck it.

"Come on, let's hit the showers, or you're going to miss the bus!" Brian said, racing to the door.

"That hurt!" I said, getting up to chase after him.

I grabbed a towel and raced into the hallway, not caring that we were both naked and still semi-hard and covered in cum. Neither of us cared, and it was early on a Saturday, so I doubted anyone would be up anyway.

"I'm going to miss you," he said as he stepped up behind me in the shower and kissed me on the shoulder.

"I'm sure you are planning an orgy while I'm gone," I joked.

"I would never," he replied in mock shock.

"I'm going to miss you too," I said, turning and pulling him close, feeling his body against mine.

"I love you," he said softly. A warm glow spread across my chest.

"I love you too," I said, kissing him deeply.

We finished showering, and I raced to pack my gear and some clothes for the trip.

"Let me know how things go with Todd," he said.

"Shit," I said.

"What?" he asked.

"I just remembered we signed up to room together on the trip," I said.

"That could get interesting," he said.

"I don't even know if he's still talking to me, and now I'm going to have to share a room with him. This is going to be awkward," I said.

"It will be okay. You can always change rooms if he's got a problem with it," he said.

"I guess you are right," I said.

"Now get out of here, or you're going to be late!" he said, smacking my butt.

I kissed him briefly before he pushed me out the door.

## CHAPTER 8

# DAVE: AWAY GAME

I was dreading this away game. I should have been excited to get to spend a night in a hotel room since it was too far to drive there and back in one day. We'd paired up for room assignments, and I'd naturally picked Todd to room with, but since the awkwardness of the other day, I was dreading seeing him, and now worse, I'd have to spend the night with him.

I walked to the bus that would take us to the other school, hypersensitive to any unusual looks I might be getting from the team that would signal he'd told them. To my relief, no one said anything.

As we boarded the bus, Todd walked past me and found a seat toward the back. I was stuck sitting with Matty. So I guess I made things weird between us after all. Fuck!

"You ready for this, Meat?" Matty said, sitting down next to me and man spreading into my space.

"Yeah, we're going to kick their asses," I said, though I was anything but confident of that.

"Fuck yeah," he yelled, slapping my thigh. He was always just a little too physical, not that I thought he was gay or anything. I just didn't know how to react. If I was physical back to him, would he somehow misinterpreted it? Would I do something wrong that revealed how much I liked dick now? If I didn't react at all, would that too be a sign? It had me on edge because Matty was always using the word "Faggot" and other choice slurs to refer to people, places, and things.

His hand lingered on my thigh for a minute too long before he turned his body toward the aisle and started chatting to Thomas about this new chick he was banging.

"She is so fucking hot, big titties, and the perfect shave pussy," he said, grabbing his crotch. His hand seemed perpetually glued to his dick. If he wasn't grabbing it over his shorts, his hand was inside the waistband fondling his shaft or balls. I knew his dick wasn't that big from the showers, but I also knew his balls were enormous and hairy making the mound of his crotch stand out.

The rhythm of the highway bumps were getting to me. My dick was semi-hard already. It was hard to hide, especially from Matty.

"Don't let her see what Meat's packing, she'll never go back to your tiny dick," Thomas joked as they both looked down at my crotch.

"Nah, a piece that big is impractical, she'll be all, 'it hurts', 'not tonight I'm too sore from last time'," he said.

"I've never had any complaints," I interjected.

"Your right hand can't complain much," Matty laughed, "when are you gonna get a girlfriend?"

"I'm not ready to be tied down," I said, though I actually was already tied down to Brian, but nobody on the team needed to know that. I wondered if Todd heard our conversation from the back. What would he think of it?

Things quieted down after a while as the bus drove on for hours. I nodded off for a bit after getting so little sleep last night. About halfway there we stopped for lunch and to stretch at a rest stop. I desperately had to piss. I headed into the plain-looking block concrete building and found an open urinal along the far wall. It was an old-school one with no dividers and urinals spaced so that you felt like you were shoulder to shoulder with the next guy.

An older guy came in and took the one next to me even though there were plenty of others further down. He pulled out his dick and waited to start. He looked down at my dick not trying to hide the fact that he was looking. It was obvious he was cruising. He tugged on his dick a few times letting it grow. I couldn't help it when mine began to fill out as well.

"Nice!" He whispered. It was just the two of us in there at the moment but it was a busy place so someone, including one of my teammates, could walk in at any moment. He reached over and grabbed hold of my dick before I could stop him.

"Fuck! And thick too!" He said. I looked around in a panic but I was frozen in place.

"Meet me in the handicap stall," he said as he put his dick away and went to the sink.

"Tell me you aren't jerking off at the urinal," Matty said, taking up a spot down from me. I felt flush in the face. I tried to hide my nearly hard cock, but Matty had already seen it. He pulled his out and let it sit atop his big balls as he started to piss. I hadn't even started to piss, but I put my dick away and headed to the sink.

I saw the older guy head to the handicap stall, but I turned and headed out, my bladder still aching for relief. I grabbed a sandwich and a water from the cooler Coach had brought and found a picnic table.

I ate my sandwich, waited for Matty and the stranger to come out so I could go finish peeing. I saw a few others go in and leave before the stranger came out, looking around. He spotted me, but I looked away embarrassed. I spotted him heading toward the parking lot. A short time later, Matty finally came out. My bladder was set to explode so I sneaked around the building and went back in, this time finally able to piss in peace. Out of curiosity, I took a peek inside the handicap stall. There was graffiti of exploding dicks on the walls and what looked like fresh cum running down the side of the divider. I guess my friend had taken care of himself.

I made my way back to the group, taking the long way. I returned in time to see Coach packing up the lunch and getting ready to hit the road again. Todd still seemed to be avoiding me. Thankfully, Matty sat with Thomas for the rest of the trip, leaving me to have a seat to myself. I thought about the stranger and what might have happened if Matty hadn't interrupted us. My dick was still semi-hard and feeling the road vibrations. I needed some relief, and I bet he would have at least given me a decent blowjob. Given I'd be sharing with Todd, I might not get a chance to even jack off later.

I nodded off again and was startled awake by something smacking me in the crotch. I looked up to find Matty standing over me laughing hysterically.

"Dreaming about Todd's ass?" he taunted. I was rock hard and it was obvious, even some precum had leaked into my shorts. Matty had spotted it and smacked it and my balls. "Nah, I preferred big butts like your's, Todd's is too skinny," I taunted back. Matty got red in the face.

"No fucking way that's going anywhere near my ass!" He said quickly going up the aisle toward the exit. I grabbed my bag and waited for the rest of the team to stream out of the bus. Todd walked past looking away from me without a glance in my direction.

We got dressed in the strange locker room and headed out to do some warm-ups before the game. Coach sat us down for the talk before the game, and then it was on.

It was a close game and tied 1 to 1 for most of it until the second half when they scored.

We tried to tie up the game. I was open, and Todd had the ball. Instead of kicking it to me, he kicked it over to Matty instead. Matty failed to make a goal I could have easily gotten in from where I was. The coach even called him on it after the game.

Defeated, we headed into the locker room, muddy from the rains the night before and the state of the field. I stripped off my kit, grabbed a towel, and headed into the shower.

"Meat," Matty greeted me at the shower entrance with a smack of my ass. I glanced over at him.

"You okay, man?" He said, seeming to sense my mood.

"Yeah," I said unconvincingly.

"What did Todd break up with you or something?" Matty asked with a laugh. I turned and punched him on the shoulder. Not hard, mind you.

"I don't know what's wrong with him," I said.

"I know. You were in a much better position to make that goal," he admitted.

"Yeah, right," I said.

I shrugged and soaped up my body, letting the mud on my legs splatter to the floor and create a dark line that circled the drain.

The image of the team lined up and stroking while they waited their turn inexplicably popped into my head. My dick began to fluff up at the idea of all those hard dicks aiming at me. I bit the inside of my cheek harder than I'd intended and tasted iron in my mouth.

"You never tell us about any of your exploits. I bet with equipment like that," Matty said. Again, he was talking about my junk. You had to wonder about some of these "straight guys" that seemed just a little too interested in other guys' dicks.

"Not much to tell, really," I lied.

"It's a pity that big dick is wasted on you," he said.

"You want it?" I said, seeing if he would take the bait. The comment seemed to go right past him.

"I would kill to have a dick like that, but that's okay, it's all in the technique anyway," he said, gyrating his hips like he was fucking some invisible pussy in front of him. His little dick bounced around uncontrollably. I seriously doubted any amount of technique made up for his little dick and bad personality. He did a little show for the rest of the shower room, and while he was turned away, I got a good look at his big round hairy ass flexing with each mock thrust. His ass was a much better asset than his dick was. If he were gay, he'd make an amazing bottom.

I pictured my dick splitting open his hairy hole and him begging me to stop. Or better yet, him begging me not to stop. I smirked at this image, thinking a good fucking by a big dick would set him straight. Or maybe not so straight as the case may be.

I finished my shower, managing to somehow keep my dick from getting fully hard. Being fluffed up was okay since it only perpetuated my nickname.

I toweled off and got dressed, looking over expecting Todd to be there at the locker next to mine, my heart sinking. I'd ruined our friendship for good this time, I thought, leaving with my bag over my shoulder.

Todd was still in his muddy kit waiting for us by the bus. He was in an especially foul mood. The whole team knew he'd blown the game with that play. He knew it too. He'd skipped the shower to avoid having to face us.

We boarded the bus, nobody saying anything. The motel on the edge of campus was a bit of a dump. Coach apologized, saying he never stayed here before but that it looked better in the pictures online. He handed out the key cards to each of us.

"Now I don't want you all to disturb the other guests. Go get settled in and meet back here in 30 minutes for dinner," Coach said before we split up to find our room.

"Hey," I said, spotting Todd at the door to 114.

"Hey," he said coldly.

"Sorry about the other night," I said. Todd looked around, spotting a couple of teammates heading up the hallway, and gave me a look like it was not okay to talk about it now. He pushed the door open into the stale, warm air of the room. I checked the thermostat. It didn't seem to be working. The ancient looking A/C unit under the window seemed to only be adding more warm air to the room.

"I'm going to take a shower before dinner," Todd said dropping his bag on the bed closest to the bathroom.

"Okay," I said, reluctantly taking the bed by the window. I ached all over. It had been a hard-fought game, but to lose after so much effort made it that much harder. I heard the shower come on and laid back across the bed, waiting for Todd to finish.

I tried to think of something to say. At least he didn't switch room assignments. That was at least some positive sign, right? I was tempted to quickly jerk off to release some stress, but I didn't want to make things any more awkward between us.

I heard the door open, and Todd emerged wearing a towel around his waist. His long, blond hair was still damp and hanging down to his shoulders. In the silhouette of the light from the bathroom, he looked like a woman.

 I adjusted my dick to make it less obvious as Todd busied himself looking through his backpack for clean clothes. Still seeming to ignore me. I felt like he didn't want me there, so I got up to leave and let him get dressed in private.

"I'm not gay," he said. Finally, some acknowledgment of what happened.  I turned to face him.

"OK, listen, I'm sorry I misread the situation the other night," I said.

"Did I do something that made you think I was gay?" He asked, his voice sharp, uncharacteristic of his normal laid-back demeanor.

"No," I lied. Of course, there were signs: him looking at my dick all the time, him popping a boner from looking at my dick, our conversation about gay blowjobs. Should I go on? It had all let up to that moment. He hadn't even objected to my touching him at the time. I was the one that freaked out.

"I can see how you might have misinterpreted things looking back on it," he said softening his tone a little.

"Yeah, I was just excited to be able to talk to you about it and got carried away," I said.

"Yeah, I may be straight but I'm not a homophobic asshole like Matty," he said.

"We cool?" I finally asked, holding out my hand.

"Yeah, we cool," he said, taking my extended hand and bumping my shoulder. He lingered a little too long before letting go.

I sat down on his bed as he picked out shorts and underwear. He looked down at me, then dropped the towel. I looked up at his semi-hard dick at eye level for a moment. Talk about mixed signals. I turned my head away and found I was still staring at his dick, this time in the mirror.

There was this moment when time seemed to stand still. He caught my eye in the mirror, and I saw his dick thickening. I wanted to just pull him toward the bed and take him down my throat, but I was worried about how he would react. The moment passed, and he pulled on his underwear. The bulge of his cock against the tight material made my mouth water.

"We're going to be late for dinner," Todd said, pulling up his jeans. I shook myself out of the daze I was in and tried to tamp down my growing dick.

# CHAPTER 9
# DAVE: SKINNY DIPPING

"I probably would have missed the goal even if you had passed to me," I said, trying to cheer up Todd. It was clear he felt bad about losing the game. It really wasn't his fault. We were both good teams, and it was a good game.

"Yeah, don't be too hard on yourself. We'll have another shot at beating them when they come to us in a couple of weeks," Coach said. We'd practically taken over the little restaurant around the corner from the motel. I was tempted to order a beer, but I didn't think Coach would approve.

We talked about the game, school, and girls, over some decent food before calling it a night. Some of the guys said they were going to check out the indoor pool at the motel; others hinted at sneaking out to go find a place to party.

"I didn't bring any swim trunks," Todd said when I asked if he wanted to go for a swim with a couple of the guys. Though he seemed to be in a little better mood after dinner, I could tell something was still bothering him.

"I'm just going to wear a pair of boxers," I said.

"I only have briefs," he said.

"You can borrow a pair of mine. I always bring extra underwear," I said.

"Uh, okay," he said hesitantly.

He headed back to the room to get changed and grab some towels.

I handed him my boxers, then stripped naked. I caught Todd glancing at my body in the mirror, but I pretended not to notice. I lingered naked to give him more time to check out my body. I went and got towels before finally putting on my boxers.

"These aren't going to work," Todd said, holding up the waistband. Todd was not as thick around the middle as I was, so the boxers were loose on him.

"They'll be okay. Once you're in the water, no one will notice," I reassured him.

He wrapped the towel around his waist anyway, then we headed down hall following the smell of chlorine.

On the way, I spotted Matty. I hoped he wasn't heading to the pool. At the last minute, he headed down another corridor toward where Coach and a few of the guys were staying. I assumed they must be getting ready to go out to the bars.

 Bull and Tommy were already in the pool, splashing around, but no one else from the hotel was there. I kicked off my shoes and waded into the water. I'd not been swimming since the campground with Brian. It felt weird to have my boxers on as I waded into the water. Swimming nude was so much better. Back in Africa, we'd swim naked all the time, just had to watch out for what else might be swimming with you.

Todd walked over to the edge of the pool, still holding the waistband of the boxers. Through the fly, I could see his soft dick peeking out. I was glad no families were around, but it was late, and they would be in bed by now. The water was actually nice and warm, probably heated since it was beginning to cool down in the evenings.

Todd was still standing on the stairs, looking like he might back out at any moment. I swam over to Todd and grabbed him around the waist, plunging him into the water. We wrestled around before he slipped out of my grasp. He emerged red in the face. Tommy and Bull started laughing.

"What the fuck!" Todd yelled.

"You wanna piece of me," I taunted him.

He lunged forward and grabbed me, throwing me off balance. I toppled backward into the water with him on top of me. I reached down to grab at him and found I was holding onto something soft and playable. He launched himself away from me, and I let go of what I now realized was his cock. When he lunged forward, the boxers he'd been wearing were pulled down by the water's resistance. He quickly pulled them up, growing bright red.

Bull and Tommy broke out in laughter, having witnessed the whole thing. I just hoped they hadn't been able to see me tugging on Todd's dick.

Todd shot a look at me of both embarrassment and confusion.

"Sorry, I guess they are a little too big on you," I said.

Todd held the waistband balled in his clenched fist and charged at me again. I braced for impact, but instead, he dove under, and I felt my boxers give way. His momentum carried forward, knocking me over. I felt the boxers tear away from me. I was now completely naked, standing in this nondescript hotel pool, with three of my teammates now turned to me, pointing, and laughing.

"Now what are you going to do?" Todd shouted, holding up my dripping boxers.

I lunged forward to grab them, but Todd hurled them across the room. They hit the window overlooking out on a courtyard in the middle of the building and slid down almost in slow motion.

"Fuck," I cried, lunging at Todd, "I'm gonna get you for that!"

He tried to run away, but I was on him in a flash. He twisted and turned under the water, still gripping the waistband of my boxers to hold them on. I tugged at them, trying to pry them free from his grip. Then I grabbed his dick intentionally this time, and he yelped.

I discovered his dick was rock hard and pushing out through the fly. I held it for a moment before he lost his grip on the waistband, and I pulled down hard. His hard dick remained the only impediment to me pulling them all the way off him. He tried to swim away, but I grabbed him and exposed his lily-white ass as the boxers pulled down. Tommy and Bull laughed and slapped the water, egging me on. They could see my bare ass facing them as I tugged and then finally something gave. I think it was the seams of my boxers because I found I was now holding on to shreds of wet cloth.

"What the fuck!" Todd cried, trying to hold a scrap of what was left of my boxers in front of his hard dick.

"Oops, sorry about that," I said, handing him the rest of the material I was holding. I stood there naked, enjoying the feeling of freedom and the warm water swirling around my bare skin.

"You're crazy, Meat!" Bull said.

"It's not the first time I've gone skinny dipping," I said as I swam lazily to the other wall and turned onto my back, floating to the surface. My dick briefly breached the surface like the periscope on a submarine.

The two spotted it and burst out laughing again. Todd just stood there trying to retain a semblance of his modesty.

"Relax, it's late and I doubt anyone else will be coming in to swim. It feels good. I used to swim naked all the time back in Swaziland," I said. Todd shook his head but a smirk formed on his lips. He laughed a nervous laugh then tossed the tattered scraps of clothes onto the side of the pool where they landed with a wet thud.

He ducked lower into the water trying to keep his dick out of sight. He seemed to finally relax and start to enjoy himself.

"You guys should join us," I said to Bull and Tommy, who looked at each other then down into the water at our naked bodies. Bull was the first to shuck his shorts, holding them high over his head before depositing them on the lip of the pool.

"At a boy," I cried as he paraded around the edge of the pool.

Tommy looked around nervously not sure what to do.

"Come on, join us," I said lightheartedly.

"Nah," he said backing into a corner.

"Suit yourself," I told him, "feels good doesn't it?"

"Yeah, we used to sneak into our neighbor's pool late at night and go skinny dipping," Bull said swimming around casually. We'd all seen each other naked so it was no big deal to be naked around each other now.

Bull was his nickname but honestly I'd forgotten what his real name was. He was a big guy, muscular with a shaved head. His body was smooth though I suspected he shaved since even his pubes were not visible.

"Okay fine," Tommy said holding up his wet shorts.

"See no big deal," I said. He kept hold of his shorts like a lifeline though, as he swam around the deeper end of the pool.

"Damn I wish Angela was here," Bull said noticeably tugging at his junk under the water. Angela was his girlfriend, a voluptuous brunette I'd seen him making out with on the quad on more than one occasion.

"You think she'd get naked with us?" Tommy asked.

"I'd send you all to bed, and we'd enjoy a little swim alone," Bull said, miming he was fucking her up against the wall.

"Debbie would never do that," Tommy said, "She wants to wait to get married."

"Fuck that, you need to dump her and find some nice pussy," Bull said, then added, "like Daniella. Bet she is a minx in bed."

Todd blushed, but then he looked down into the water with a hint of longing on his face. It was difficult to see clearly through the water, but I guessed that both Bull and Tommy were just as hard now as Todd and I were.

"Damn, I wish she was here, fuck!" Bull said, slapping his dick under the water so that you could almost feel the muffled sound of it.

"You'd better watch out tonight," I said to Tommy, knowing that they were rooming together.

"I'm not that desperate," Bull said, looking over at Tommy. Tommy gave a nervous laugh.

"You could get in big trouble doing that here," came a new voice from the doorway.

We all looked up to find the man that had checked us in earlier standing in the doorway, looking down into the water and our shed clothing. He was a young guy, maybe in his late twenties, a little overweight, with a full beard and hair that was beginning to thin on top.

"Oh shit," Tommy said, frantically trying to pull his trunks back on. Todd swam to the other side to retrieve what was left of my boxers and Bull swam over and grabbed his shorts.

I just stood there in the water, gazing at the interloper. I was nearly certain by the way he looked at all of us when we checked in, that we was checking us out. I was sure he was gay. I knew he had to do his job, but I had a feeling he didn't mind the fact that there were four hot college guys swimming naked in the pool.

"It's late. I don't think anyone will complain," I said, walking slowly up the stairs closest to him. His mouth fell open slightly, and he let out an audible gasp as his eyes fell on my semi-hard member. My suspicions were correct. Licked his lips like he was ready to drop to his knees and worship my cock. It looked like he might know what he was doing. I might have to find a way to sneak out later and put that additional theory to the test.

He seemed lost for words as he stared at my cock swinging back and forth as I walked slowly past him, then to the spot where my boxers sat below the window.

I held them up and wrung them out before walking back past him to retrieve my towel. Again, his eyes were glued to my cock as he stood there mesmerized.

The others had already scrambled out of the pool and were quickly drying off. Todd stood with his towel wrapped tightly around his waist. The bulge of his hard dick pressed into the terrycloth obscenely.

I wished I could have caught a better glimpse of Bull and Tommy before they got out, especially to see what they looked like hard, but they were already dressed and making for the exit in a hurry while I distracted the clerk, who's name tag read "Peter".

"Sorry if we got you in trouble," I said, holding up my towel behind my back, facing Peter so he could have another good, long look at my body and my hard dick.

"No, it's okay. I just don't want anyone to complain," he said, his voice cracking as he addressed me, well, actually my dick since he never took his eyes off of it.

"Well, have a nice evening," I said as I finally wrapping the towel around my waist and cinching it into a tight knot. I hung my boxers on my shoulder and walked past the him once more, heading toward the exit. Todd quickly fled past me into the corridor, forgetting to grab the tatters of my boxers.

I went back and picked them up to. Now I was alone in the pool room with the Peter. Only the sound of the still sloshing water could be heard as I walked back toward him.

"Are you working the desk all night?" I asked casually.

"Till 6," he gulped.

"Maybe I'll stop by later to more formally apologize," I said, taking hold of his hand. Like I was going to shake on it, but then brought it closer to my bulge. He whimpered as his fingers traced the outline of my cock in the fabric.

"Fuck!" He breathed.

"See you later," I said, as I walked past him, checking out his wide ass as I passed.

## CHAPTER 10

# DAVE: CONCIERGE

"Holy shit," Todd said when I caught up with him on the way back to our room. He was with Bull and Tommy. Their room was a little further down the hall.

"I know, I thought we were dead," Tommy said.

"Nah, we're fine. I made sure he's not going to report us," I said. I will make sure of that when I give him my load later, I thought. I don't know what got into me back there. I felt so confident, which seemed totally out of character for me. I loved how the guy was like clay in my hands.

"That was too close," Tommy said.

"What'd you say to him?" Bull asked.

"I played up my accent and told him where I come from we swim in the nude. He was very understanding," I said.

"That's because he wants your Meat," Bull said looking down at The impression of it in my towel.

"You think so?" I asked, like I was totally oblivious to that obvious fact.

"If eyes could fuck, he'd be having your babies," Bull said, laughing.

"I didn't know. Maybe that's why he was so nice about it," I lied pretending I was that naive.

"It was fun while it lasted," Bull said, grinning.

"Yeah, it was," I said.

"See you boys in the morning," Bull said, turning to head down the hall toward their room.

"Good night," I said, making silly kissy noises in their direction that only straight guys can get away with doing between each other.

As soon as the door closed behind us, I pulled off the towel, hung it and my wet boxers over the shower door, and walked over to my bed. The room was still sweltering. It seemed like the heat was on. It didn't mind it so much after being wet and in the overly cold hallway.

I tapped the temperature controls, but it didn't seem to change anything.

"I might have to go down and see if the clerk can get maintenance up here to fix it," I said, looking for a plausible excuse to go visit my new friend.

"It's okay for now," Todd said, still in his damp towel, sitting on the edge of his bed.

"You don't mind if I sleep like this? I would sleep in my boxers, but ..." I trailed off.

"It's fine," Todd said, with forced casualness in his voice.

"That was fun," I said, flopping down on the bed. My dick fell heavily against my thigh, and I left it there.

Todd clicked off his light, plunging the room into darkness. The curtains were open, letting in the amber glow of the lights from the parking lot. As my eyes adjusted to the dim light, I saw that Todd had taken off his towel and was lying on top of his bed. It was too warm in the room to even pull on a sheet.

"I've never done anything like that," Todd said.

"You've never gone skinny dipping?" I asked.

"No, we have a pool at home but my dad keeps the lights on it all the time, I would never get away with it," Todd said. I could just make out the shape of his dick, looking plump as it rested against his abs.

"Like I said I grew up swimming naked, it was the norm over there," I said.

"I can't believe how calm you were about getting caught, I'm still shaking," he said.

"I know, I'm surprise myself," I said.

"You must have known he was gay, right?" He asked seeing through the lie I'd told Bull.

"I had my suspicions, I figured he must have been watching us on the camera," I said.

"There was a camera? Oh fuck!" Todd said sounding a little more panicked now.

"Don't worry. Like I said he isn't about to report us," I reassured him.

I heard Todd sigh in relief. He was quiet for a moment like there was something more he wanted to say but left it unsaid. The room was quiet except for the clicking of the broken a/c unit and the compressor on the mini fridge kicking on and off periodically.

Was I feeling tension between us, or was it just my imagination? I couldn't tell if he was looking over at me, but I could see his dick hardening. My dick began to harden too in response. I reached down and gave it the briefest tug. I could easily just pass it off as adjusting myself. I waited to see if Todd returned the gesture. His dick jumped again, rising and falling against his abs until it lifted completely off of them to float above them like the assistant in a magic trick.

I tugged my dick again, letting it arch up over my abs as well. The illumination from the outside lights was brighter on my side of the room, so if he was watching, he would know I was rock hard now. His face was in shadow, so I couldn't gauge his reactions.

I pulled on my cock once more, this time lingering with my hand holding it. I caught movement with Todd's bed. I could see his hand reaching down to grab hold of his cock.

Slowly, I began to stroke the full length of my shaft, exaggerating my normal technique, hoping that Todd was watching. I was fairly confident that he was when he began to match my movements, tugging on his dick. I ran my fingers through the hair on my belly and up through my chest hair to find my sensitive nipple. I tugged on it and pulled on my balls, letting my dick sway in the air. I was definitely putting on a show for Todd, and he seemed to be a receptive audience.

I wanted desperately to get out of my bed and go over to him, but I was afraid to break the spell and freak him out. Even if we could just be JO buddies, I'd be okay with that. I know it takes time to overcome societal pressures and your own hang-ups.

I began to stroke myself faster, pinching my nipple, as precum began to leak from my wide piss slit. I wished I could get a closer look at Todd as he also began to pick up the pace. I should hear his heavy breathing now, and I could catch a whiff of his musky scent over the stronger odor of chlorine.

I could hear Todd's bed creaking as his body shook with the pounding he was giving his dick. I could hear the slapping of his wet skin as his precum-coated foreskin retracted over his head over and over again.

"Oh shit," Todd gasped, and I caught the glint of the streetlamp illuminating splotches of wetness appearing on his chest and abdomen. His abs tightened, and his toes curled as he fucked his hand. The wet slapping grew louder as he sent multiple streams into the air. I watched, stroking my dick, getting close but not close enough to join him right away. He stopped stroking and let his dick fall to his abs with a wet slap. I continued to stroke, wishing I was there licking the cum off his chest and abs. I heard the bed squeak and saw Todd moving toward the bathroom. For a brief moment, I caught his silhouette against the bright rectangle of the bathroom door before the door closed, and I heard the shower come on.

I knew the excitement was over for the evening, at least where Todd was concerned. He would finish his shower and go straight into post-nut slumber. He'd probably forget the whole incident in the morning.

I got up while he was in the shower and pulled on my sweatpants and a t-shirt. I grabbed my room card and slipped out of the room into the bright corridor.

"Just getting back from the club?" I asked when I surprisingly ran into Matty coming down the corridor. He looked up, a look of something like panic on his face. I think he didn't expect to see anyone out this late.

"Uh ... yeah, just got back," he said, recovering. "Had a wild time."

"You'll have to tell me all about it on the bus," I said.

"What are you doing up?" He asked.

"Heading to the vending machines to get a soda. The a/c is busted, and I can't sleep. Maybe I'll see if they can send someone up to fix it," I said.

"Damn that sucks. This place is a dump. Just don't let that faggot manning the front get into your pants," he said.

That's exactly what I planned on letting him do, I thought. "Yeah, Bull already warned me," I said instead.

"How was the pool?" He asked.

"The pool was alright. It was too warm to be refreshing," I said.

"Oh yeah, a swim did sound nice to cool off, but maybe not," he said.

"I think it's closed by now. We got kicked out," I said.

"Oh," he said.

"I'll see you tomorrow," I said, walking on.

"Yeah, night, Meat," he said.

I made sure he wasn't following me before heading away from the vending machines and toward the front desk.

"Evening," I said to Peter.

"Evening," he said, looking up from his book. When he realized who it was, he sat up at attention.

"Was nice to meet you earlier. I was hoping maybe ..." I said.

"I've got to man the desk in case anyone comes in," he said.

"You get a break to go to the bathroom, don't you?" I said.

"Yeah, I guess I could," he said. I grabbed my unsatisfied cock through the thin material. He looked down at the clear outline of my head and shaft pointing out. He looked around nervously, then nodded toward the camera mounted behind the counter. I got his meaning and let go.

He then nodded toward the sign for the bathroom, just around the corner from the lobby.

"Hope you have a good evening," I said before heading over in the direction of the bathroom. I ducked inside and waited. I pulled out my dick and began to stroke it back to full hardness. A few minutes later, I heard the door squeak open as Peter came in. He looked down and once again let out an audible gasp. He reached back and flipped the deadbolt into place, then was on his knees in seconds.

His warm mouth engulfed my cock to the base with no problem. I was right, he knew how to give head. I guessed I wasn't the first guest to take advantage of his generous throat. He expertly sucked my dick, stroking my shaft with his wet hand as he focused on the upper part of my shaft and head with his tongue. I grabbed the back of his head to steady myself more than to tell him what to do. He was doing an excellent job without any coaching.

I thought about Todd and watching him cum all over his chest, and I got closer to giving Peter my load. He sensed I was close and backed off.

"You fuck?" He asked. I thought for a second, then nodded.

"Fuck me," he said, standing and heading toward the sinks. He undid his belt and let his dress pants fall around his black socked ankles. He pulled up his shirt and bent forward over the sinks to reveal a wide, hairy ass with a thick strip of hair running up the center and an inviting-looking pucker winking its readiness to receive my load. I stepped out of my sweats and got up behind him. I let a line of spit fall into his crack and roll over his hole, though it didn't look like it needed any extra lube. It seemed like he was already prepped and ready to take my cock.

I slapped his ass a few times and teased his hole.

"You want this big, fat dick?" I asked.

"Yes, please!" He said, pulling his cheeks apart to widen his hole and draw me in. Something I never thought I'd ever be doing a few months ago, fucking a strange man in a bathroom. He had me so turned on. I pressed my wide head into his hole.

"Oh fuck you are thick," he said, trying to quickly adapt. I kept up the pressure and then suddenly popped inside.

"Oh fuck!" He cried, holding on to the counter with white knuckles.

"Damn you feel good," I said, sinking slowly inside him. I had to pick up the pace or I was likely to cum on my first stroke. I was already overly sensitive and out of my mind at what had happened at the pool, then in the room with Todd.

"Oh yeah! Fuck me hard, give me your fucking load," he said, pushing out his ass to back up on my cock to the base. I realized he didn't have much time either before he might be missed at the front desk. Though it was late, there was always the chance that someone would still check in or need something.

I pounded out my frustrations on Peter. His ass took them, his wide ass jiggling each time I landed a stroke deep inside him. I was ready to shoot, there was no stopping it now.

"Oh fuck, I'm gonna cum," I said, unsure of the protocol, should I pull out, should I shoot it inside him?

"Breed me, give me that big load!" He gasped.

"Fuck!", I yelled, maybe a bit too loudly and did just that. I filled his hole with my worked-up load. My balls ached as they churned out jet after jet of cum. I fell against his back, sweat gluing me to him. I felt his ass clench and massage my dick nearly to the point of expelling it.

"Oh fuck," he gasped as his ass fluttered and clamped down hard. When he'd finally calmed down, relaxing against the counter top, I slowly pulled out, leaving a trail of cum that dripped off his balls and onto his dress pants.

I helped him stand and saw the puddle of cum on the counter a few inches from the sink. I'd fucked a nice big load out of him.

"Holy fuck that was hot," he said, regaining his breath and standing.

"Yeah, it was," I said.

"Listen, could you not say anything about this, my teammates don't know," I said.

"Are you straight?" He asked.

"No, not really, not anymore, but I'm not open about it, especially with these guys," I said.

"It's a hot group of guys, you a team?" He asked.

"Yeah, football ... I mean soccer," I said.

"Nice. If anyone else on the team needs some release, you can send them my way. I can be discreet," he said.

"Too bad we are leaving in the morning. Maybe next away game," I said, knowing we wouldn't be back, at least not this season.

"Too bad. I'd love to take all of your loads, woof," he said, pawing at my hairy chest. I leaned down and kissed him, which I think surprised him. "Fuck, I wish I could stay with you in here all night. You could fuck me for hours if you wanted," he said.

"But you'd better get back to the desk. I don't want you to lose your job," I told him, giving him one more kiss. His lips were soft and tasted like coconut lip balm.

"Yeah, it sucks. Okay, good night," he said, zipping up his pants and cinching his belt in place. He reached back and unlocked the door.

"Wait five minutes, then leave down the corridor," he cautioned me.

"Okay, good night," I said, smiling.

After waiting five minutes, I left without going past the desk. I had to loop around to get back to my room, but I didn't want to get Peter in trouble if they were monitoring him using the cameras.

I heard Todd snoring when I came in. He had the thin sheet pulled up over him. It appeared the a/c had kicked in a little bit, but it was still too warm for me to sleep in anything. I took a quick shower, fumbling around in the dark so I wouldn't disturb Todd.

I got into bed and fell asleep quickly. I don't know what time it was, but I knew Coach would be rousing us early to grab breakfast and hit the road in the morning.

## CHAPTER 11

# DAVE: EARLY RISERS

It was late, but Todd and I decided to go back down to the pool for another swim. This time we didn't bother to put on anything, just got in naked. The warm water felt so nice on my aching muscles. Just then I felt something brush against my leg and found Todd swimming up to me. His hand moved up my leg toward my hardening dick. Then he was on it, his mouth sinking down my pole under the water. The feeling of his mouth and the water had me on edge.

"Looks like someone else had the same idea," came a voice from the entrance to the pool. I looked up to find Bull and Tommy standing by the wall. Tommy was down on his knees in front of Bull, lapping at his thick cock. Todd came up for air and gasped when he saw them standing there.

"Oh shit," he said.

"Relax, we're cool. After we got back to our room Tommy confessed he wanted to suck my dick," Bull said, holding Tommy's head in place and skull fucking him. I had Todd get up on the side of the pool and sank down on his cock. It was what I had wanted to do all season, and now I finally had it in my mouth. I studied every inch of it with my tongue as he moaned in delight.

"Time to get up!" I heard someone shouting. I saw Coach with Matty not far behind, round the corner, to find us there.

I opened my eyes when I heard the pounding on the door. Todd was standing over me, looking down at my massive morning wood. He was in the process of trying to stuff his morning wood into a pair of shorts before answering the door. Had he just been standing there looking at my hard dick while I slept? I saw a wet spot form on the front of his shorts where his dick pushed against the fabric, trying to escape.

"We're up," he said, opening the door just a crack to talk to Coach.

"Okay, meet in the lobby in 15 minutes," Coach said before Todd let the door close and headed back into the room.

"You okay if I jump in the shower first?" He asked.

"Sure, no problem," I said pulling the sheet over my dick, feeling like it was making things awkward again. The sheet only made it look like I'd pitched a tent in the middle of the room. I rolled onto my side as Todd turned and headed into the bathroom. Nothing was said about last night, or the fact that we'd jerked off just feet from each other. I almost didn't think it was real until I spotted a crusty spot on his comforter. I brought it to my nose and took a deep inhale of his scent.

My bladder suddenly reminded me of its existence. I heard the shower come on and tried to hold it, but I was finding it hard to.

"Okay, if I come in to take a piss?" I asked.

"Um, okay," Todd said.

The shower was a bathtub with a glass sliding door on it. I could see Todd turn away quickly when I entered, but he couldn't hide the shadow of his hard cock on the wall behind him. I stood at the toilet just in front of the shower, willing my cock to go down enough for me to piss. I could feel eyes on me, but I tried not to look over at him.

Finally, my bladder overrode my throbbing cock, and I let loose a torrent into the bowl. I relaxed, and a shiver ran down my spine. When I was done, I tugged a few times, getting the last few drops from my shaft. I still had that sense that Todd was watching. I turned to leave, and I saw him shift, trying to hide his erection from me. I managed to catch a glimpse of it anyway. It was much stiffer today than that time in the shower. It arched up in front of him toward the left of his abs. His smooth crotch and balls only made it look bigger, but I knew I had at least 2 inches in length and quite a bit of girth on him. It was still a nice, mouthwatering cock to look at.

I kept walking, my dick swinging and slapping my legs with each step. We didn't have much time left, so I opted to skip the shower and get dressed.

'I'll meet you down there," I called out to Todd, who hadn't gotten out of the shower yet. I didn't have to wondered what he was doing in there. Maybe this time he wouldn't refuse my offer to help if I went back in there. I dismissed the thought. Baby steps, we jacked off together, so that was something. Maybe he would be open to doing more in time, but I wasn't counting on it.

We'd have a chance to grab our bags after breakfast, so I left my packed bag by the door and headed downstairs, leaving Todd to finish his shower and dress in privacy. Coach and Matty were waiting for us. Soon, the others trickled in. Bull and Tommy walked in together, and I caught Tommy grinning at Bull. Then he saw me and gave me a little smirk. I'd hoped to see Peter again, but the front desk was manned by a black woman with some of the biggest breasts I'd ever seen. I was surprised she didn't fall over forward from the weight of them.

"Is Todd going to be joining us?" Coach asked me.

"He was in the shower when I left, but he should be down shortly," I said.

"Bet I know what he's doing," Matty said, making a rude gesture to a murmur of giggles. I was sure that was exactly what he was doing, but I wasn't going to say.

"You're late," Coach said as Todd wandered in five minutes later.

"Sorry, I lost track of time getting ready," Todd apologized.

"Had to clean up the mess you made," Matty said, making the same gesture. Todd's face reddened.

"Okay that's enough. Let's eat and then hit the road," Coach said giving Matty a menacing look.

Attached to the hotel was a hole-in-the-wall greasy spoon with surprisingly good food. We had to split up since they didn't have a large enough tables for all of us. Todd and I sat with Bull and Tommy.

"You have a good night?" I asked. Tommy blushed at my question.

"It was a good night," Bull said, smiling.

"Still can't believe we got caught skinny dipping," Todd said, looking embarrassed. I wondered if Bull was even referring to the skinny dipping the way Tommy looked at him. It was probably just my imagination, but there seemed to be a different energy between them this morning, not unlike the first morning I woke up next to Brian in the tent. I remembered that warm, fuzzy feelings I had when I was around him. I was almost sure something had happened between them. I pictured Bull shoving his cock deep into Tommy's throat then in his ass and smiled at the coupling. Then I rearranged the image so that Bull was on all fours with Tommy rearranging Bull's guts with his surprisingly massive cock. All the skinny boys seem to hide the fact that they have massive cocks. I wished I'd gotten a closer look when they were in the pool.

"I know, that was crazy," Tommy said, looking to Bull in relief, like they shared a secret that hadn't been discovered. I let it go, thinking, good for them.

The plates cleaned and checks paid from Coach's travel budget, we made our way back to our rooms to grab our bags and hit the road.

"You should have been there," Fischer said to Matty. "We were dancing with these two chicks at the bar. They were grinding all over us!"

"I thought you went out with them?" I asked. Matty looked confused for a minute.

"Nah, I went out on my own, scored this super hot chick; we did it back at her hotel room," Matty bragged. I seriously doubted his story. Something wasn't adding up. Matty was the type to overstate his prowess with the ladies, and I suspected that was the case here. Maybe he did go out on his own but ended up striking out.

"Nice," Fischer said, raising an eyebrow like he didn't believe him either but didn't call him out on it.

"I've got this hot date lined up for tonight!" Matty said. Fischer and I looked at him incredulously.

"Met her on one of the apps," Matty said.

"Careful, she's liable to be a he," Cross piped in.

"Nah, she sent me pictures of everything, a perfect shaved pussy just waiting for my dick," he said, grabbing his crotch.

"So she'll still be waiting even after you leave her place," I piped in. Matty flashed me an angry look, but he wasn't about to pick a fight with me.

"Well, at least my meat is getting some action," he spat back, unable to find anything better to come at me with.

It was a long ride back to campus, but at least Todd was sitting next to me this time, and I didn't feel the same awkwardness as before. I messaged Brian when we were expected back.

"Who's that?" Todd asked.

"Brian," I said, "He asked if you want to come to dinner with us."

"I've got plans," he replied.

"Oh yeah," I said, brightening.

"I'm gonna treat Daniella to a romantic dinner and a movie," he said.

"Nice!" I said trying to hide my disappointment.

"I told her we weren't getting back until tomorrow, so it will really be a surprise," he said.

"You sure that's wise? Girls don't really like being lied to," I said.

"I didn't lie, I just said I wouldn't see her until Monday, probably. She assumed I would be away all weekend," he said.

"Okay," I said, doubtfully.

"We've been going through a rough patch lately. I'm just looking to do something special for her to shake things up. You know what I mean?" he said.

"Yeah, I guess I can see that. I hope you have a good time," I said, though I didn't care for Daniella much. I know being with her made Todd happy, so I tried not to be too negative.

"So, we're cool with everything," I said softly so others couldn't overhear us against the murmur of conversations and the noise of the bus. Todd looked around nervously, expecting Matty to pop up at any moment.

"Yeah, we're cool," he said, dropping the conversation there. I wanted to ask him about last night and how he felt about it, but this wasn't the time or place. I let it go, happy that I had my friend back and mostly content that we would remain just friends.

## CHAPTER 12

# JUNIOR: BROKEN HEART

I  met Dave at the door when he came in and dropped his bag by the door. I pulled him into a tight embrace.

"I missed you," I said, kissing him.

"I missed you too. I wish you had been there," he said.

"Oh, did I miss something juicy?" I said, reading the mischievous look on his face.

"You did," he said, telling me all about skinny dipping and then jacking off in the bed next to Todd. Then about the hotel clerk.

"Fuck! Why didn't you send me pictures at least!" I said, mock hitting him in the chest rather harder than I had intended.

"I didn't think about it and it was really late. I hope it was okay that I fucked him?," he said.

"Of course it is okay. I fucked Ravi last night," I told him.

"Of course you did," he said, rolling his eyes.

"He's all worked up about telling his girlfriend about his bisexuality," I said.

"I can understand that," he said. I looked at him, thinking about the fact that he was also bisexual and what that might mean for him down the road. I pushed away the thought.

He was looking hopelessly at his desk and the mountain of work he needed to get done.

"We'll get something to eat now and then get right on it when we get back," I said, nodding at my own assignments. "No sex till it's all done," I said, but who was I kidding? I'm not sure either of us could last five minutes without fucking like rabbits. But we did just that, grabbed some food, and headed back to the room to study.

He pulled off his shirt when we came in but left on his sweatpants. Even in the dead of winter, I felt like Dave would still walk around at least shirtless. He was naturally hot-blooded, and that thick pelt of hair helped keep him warm. It warmed me just looking at it. All I wanted to do was go over there and lick his perky nipples.

For hours, we focused on our work. I sat at my desk, working on my laptop while Dave read on his bed. I glanced over at him. Though I should have been focused on my assignment, I was instead focused on the trail of hair disappearing under the waistband and the bulge in his sweats. Surprisingly, I was fully clothed, as it got colder outside, our room also grew colder. I'd tried to set the thermostat on high, but the air coming out of the vent still seemed cold. Why didn't I choose a southern school where it was warm all year round?

"Get back to work," he said, causing me to jump. I looked up to find he was looking at me over the top of his book.

"I can't help it if you are sexy as fuck," I said.

"Should I put on a shirt so as not to tempt you," he said.

"Don't you dare," I said. He laughed.

Just then, there was a soft knock at the door. It was late, and we normally didn't get unannounced visitors at this hour.

I got up and went to the door.

I was surprised to find Todd standing on the other side of it. He sniffed and blinked rapidly. His eyes looked puffy and red.

"Dave in?" He croaked.

"Yeah, come on in," I said. He hesitated for a moment like he might have preferred Dave to come out, but then walked past me into the room. Dave sat up when he saw Todd.

"Yo, what's up?" Dave asked, rotating on his bed to give Todd a place to sit.

"Nothing ..." Todd said, slumping down on the bed. It definitely didn't look like nothing. You don't show up at someone's door in the middle of the night with puffy red eyes for nothing.

"You sure?" Dave asked. I sat down on my bed, looking over at Dave and Todd. Todd was wearing a button-down shirt that was now half untucked from his jeans. His eyes looked glassy, like tears were forming.

"I ... I caught her fucking ... Matty!" his eyes flashed with anger, like he was about to punch the air.

"Oh shit! Really? Matty and Daniella?" Dave asked, pointlessly. It couldn't have been anyone else.

"Yeah," Todd said, slumping down.

"Sorry, man," Dave said, trying to be supportive, but I knew he couldn't stand her. There was something about her attitude and whiny voice that got on both our nerves. She treated him like shit, making him do everything for her, and he got nothing but bitching and complaining from her in return.

"What happened? I thought you had a date planned," Dave said.

"I went over to surprise her, and that's when I heard them going at it through the door. They didn't even bother to lock it," he said, between angry sobs.

"What the fuck!" Dave said.

"I went in and found her riding him." Todd said, getting more agitated by the minute.

"Fuck that dude," Dave said, moving closer to his friend and rubbing his back. Todd began to shake and sob uncontrollably. He began to pour his heart out to us. I felt a bit uncomfortable witnessing the scene. I didn't know Todd that well, and I felt like I was intruding. Dave patted his back sympathetically.

"She didn't even care ... when I walked in on them. She looked me straight in the eye and kept riding him," Todd said, looking like he was about to punch a hole in the concrete.

"Really?! I'm sorry, dude," Dave said his fist clenching. One of the many traits I love about Dave is his fierce loyalty to his friends. He would go to war if anyone upset me and I know he would do the same for Todd.

"It was like she wanted to humiliate me," Todd said.

"That's fucked up!" Dave said. "You can do so much better. I didn't want to say anything because I know how much you liked her but she really treated you like shit," Dave said. Todd didn't seem to hear him.

"What has he got that I don't?" He wailed. The dam burst, and tears began to flow again.

"Certainly not a bigger dick, that's for sure," Dave said jokingly. Todd looked up at him, caught off guard by the comment. He sniffed back his tears and gave a tentative laugh.

"I know, right?" Todd finally said. Dave held up a pinky to illustrate for me his approximation of Matty's dick size. I giggled.

"No wonder she hasn't been putting out lately," he said.

"Fuck, dude, how long has it been?" Dave asked.

"Over a month," she said. "She said she had bad cramps from her period," he said.

"For a fucking month?" Dave said. Todd shook his head, now realizing how much she lied to him. Love is truly blind.

"You're better off without her. Now she's his problem," Dave said. Todd nodded his head in agreement.

"You'll find someone else," Dave said.

"I think I'm done with dating for a while," Todd said.

"Give it some time," Dave offered.

"I wish I was gay," Todd said, "Seems like you guys have it figured out."

"I don't know about that," Dave said. I looked at him puzzled. I thought we kinda did have it figured out. Was there something he wasn't telling me?

"Must be nice to be gay and room with your boyfriend and have sex any time you want," he said.

"It's a nice arrangement. Only wish we had a bigger bed," Dave said.

"A problem I wish I had," Todd countered.

"One thing I will say," he said, grabbing his cock in his jeans for emphasis, "She gave really good head when she did." I could see a sizable lump forming in the folds of the jeans, moving up toward the pocket.

"I bet you anything Brian gives better head than her," Dave challenged. I was shocked that Dave said it out loud. Of course, it was exactly what I was thinking. My dick started to grow and press against my sweatpants. I was not wearing any underwear. Todd was lucky I was even wearing these, given my usual attire.

Todd gave a nervous laugh, looking in my direction as if he just realized I was still in the room.

"You know the first night we roomed together, he sucked off one of our hall mates right in front of me," Dave said. I felt flush, and I'm sure I turned a deep shade of scarlet.

"Really?" Todd said. I avoided his gaze.

"Yeah, trust me, it's no exaggeration when I said he was good. I've never had one better than his," Dave said. I felt pride swell inside me. I loved his cock and did my best every time I had it in my mouth. It was nice to hear him compliment my ability in that area.

Todd shifted uncomfortably. It was clear his dick was hard by the throbbing lump in his jeans. There was an awkward silence as Todd looked down at his crotch, maybe realizing for the first time he was hard. He moved his hand in front of it to try to hide it from view. It was, of course, pointless since Dave and I had both seen it.

"I could give you a demonstration," I said before thinking. Dave shot me a look that was both fear and longing.

"Ah, I don't think ..." Dave started to say.

"I've been so horny lately, I was hoping I'd get her in the mood with dinner and a movie earlier," Todd said, looking intently at a hole in the wall where some previous tenant had tried to hammer a nail into the concrete.

Todd hadn't rejected my offer outright, but he also hadn't said yes either. I saw his dick jump, and a wet spot form in the faded denim just above the head of his trapped cock.

Todd kept staring at the wall, not looking at me or Dave.

"I'm not gay," Todd said as he cupped his dick. I could see it push back against his fingers as the wet spot in the denim spread.

"I didn't think I was either," Dave said softly. Todd's gaze stayed fixed on the wall, but he moved his hand away from his cock. It pressed against his jeans, pushing out multiple times as if saying, "Please touch me."

"You need some help with that?" I asked, getting up from my bed and kneeling down on the floor between Todd and Dave. His eyes shot down at me, then over at Dave. Dave's dick was making a giant circus tent out of his sweatpants. Todd's gaze fixed on the pulsating lump, and his cock jumped as if syncing up with the motion he was seeing.

I ran my hand up Dave's leg and gathered the fabric around the base of his cock, so you could see every contour and vein stand out against the fabric. Todd's mouth hinged open, and his dick pressed against the denim once more.

## CHAPTER 13

# JUNIOR: BROKEN BOUNDARIES

I began to stroke Dave's cock through the fabric while Todd watched, his dick ready to break through his jeans.

"This ok?" Dave asked. Todd looked up at him then back down nodding slightly as if in a daze.

I took things up a notch and pulled at the elastic. Dave's cock sprang up like trebuchet, launching precum beads at a castle wall. Todd gasped involuntarily and locked onto Dave's huge dick. I stroked it openly for him as Dave's precum began to leak down my fingers. I made a show of licking it off my fingers, savoring the taste of him. Todd squirmed as his dick jumped uncontrollably.

Dave's tilted his head back and let out an exaggerated moan as I lowered my mouth onto his shaft. I put on the best performance I could, getting Dave's dick shiny wet. Todd's eyes were fixed on my mouth and Dave's cock.

"Go on take yours out," Dave commanded in a low seductive voice. I melted hearing his voice like that. I couldn't resist it and it seemed Todd couldn't either. I heard the button on his jeans pop open and looked over to see his bright red briefs stick out from the fly. I could clearly make out the head and the dark spot his precum had made on the material. Todd looked around self consciously before pulling back the underwear and letting his dick flop down against his abs.

It was average sized but beautiful, with a tight foreskin. I licked my lips. I couldn't wait to taste that wet skin. It took all my willpower not to just go over and devour it entirely.

"Damn, that feels so good," Dave said as I pulled his skin tight and lapped at the sensitive underside of his cock. I saw movement as Todd's hand moved up and down his shaft. His balls bounced as the skin folded over the head and pulled back down.

"You wanna try?" Dave asked, nodding down at me slurping vigorously at his head. Todd seemed to think for a moment but let his dick decide for him. It bounced and oozed more precum onto his tight abs. He was shaved smooth which was somewhat disappointing. It did help his dick look bigger than it actually was.

I let go of Dave's cock and shifted toward Todd getting in between his legs. They shook involuntarily as I ran my fingers along the stitching of his jeans.

I looked up at his face for guidance but he was now watching Dave stroke his meat. Dave was using his left hand so Todd could see him better.

I reached up and took hold of Todd's dick pulling it up and admiring the steely firmness against my fingers. His muscles tensed but he didn't try to stop me. I tugged at his cock feeling the tight skin. The foreskin was so tight it resisted pulling down over his large head. I'd heard of guys getting surgery to loosen a tight foreskin like this but he'd not had it. Precum oozed down my fingers from the volcanic eruption above. His body shook as I leaned in and licked up the savory-sweet liquid.

"Oh fuck," Todd gasped as I took him in my mouth running my tongue along the sensitive skin. I put into practice the lessons I had learned sucking Kieth's uncut cock. I tried to do what I had done to him, slipping my tongue between his foreskin and head but the skin was much tighter than Kieth's. Todd whimpered and a flood of precum filled my mouth. It was clear he was pent up and ready to explode any minute. I reached down and tugged at his smooth balls which were already tucked up under him in firing position.

I caressed those big balls feeling the weight of them in my hand. He wasn't wrong, he needed them drained and on a more regular basis than he'd been getting. I felt the stubble around the base of his cock which jutted straight out from him with a slight upward and to the right angle. His shaft was smaller at the base and widened a bit before it reached the partially covered head. I tugged on it watching the skin pull back as if it was a rubber band holding his head in place. It looked painfully tight.

I watched Todd's face for signs he was having second thoughts. He was still staring off in the distance, his bright blue eyes and blond lashes catching the overhead light.

Dave got up and stood next to me stroking his cock, while watching me once again take Todd's dick in my mouth.

Todd's gaze went down to Dave's cock and his eye's widened. I'm sure Todd had seen Dave naked in the locker room plenty of times but not his hard cock inches from his face like he was seeing now. Todd looked away as if he was afraid to watch but stole glances back at it from time to time his mouth slightly open.

I closed the gap between us and stuck out my tongue to taste the bead of clear fluid that had formed at Todd's piss hole. It was salty and had just a hint of sweetness. I slipped his whole cock into my mouth all the way to the root massaging it with my throat and tongue. Todd gasped as his balls tumbled against my chin.

"Fuck!" he breathed out as I ran my tongue over the smooth tight skin and brought my lips back to the tip. I licked at it and rolled the skin back letting my tongue slip along his exposed head. Todd grunted and pulled back a little in response. He was more sensitive there then I expected. I sucked the skin back into place over his sensitive head and gently ran my tongue over the foreskin and down his shaft. This elicited a moan from Todd. I cupped his balls feeling them churning inside his sack preparing a load for me.

I let my fingers wander down a little teasing his taint. His cock jumped in my mouth flooding it with more precum as I pressed on the hard flesh just under his balls. I could tell he was close already. I let his cock go from my mouth and ran my tongue over his balls. I couldn't get them both in my mouth at once so I did one at a time, lightly sucking on each and lapping at them with my tongue. I felt Dave shift and bend down. I looked up to find him licking Todd's precum covered head.

I tugged at Todd's jeans and he obliged by lifting his ass off the bed and letting me pull them down his legs and all the way off. This gave me better access to his balls and taint. Since he had his legs up to let me take off his jeans his crack and the tight pink pucker of his rosebud were exposed. I dove in before he could object and while Dave had him distracted with his mouth on his cock. I licked down his crack and his pucker.

What came out of Todd's lips was and incoherent string of syllables resembling but not quite becoming a string of curse words. He gasped as his ass muscles tightened and flexed. I continued to lick and suck his hole. I flicked at his opening with my tongue just getting a little bit inside him. The musk smell coming off his ass was even stronger than his crotch. It made me want to lick him more. He actually pulled up his legs to let me get in deeper. He gasped and whimpered continuously as I invaded his most private sector.

I went back to licking his balls then joined Dave licking up his shaft. We licked up the side of his shaft together almost kissing each other in the process. Dave sat back on the bed and stroked his cock watching me suck his straight teammate.

Todd surprised us both by reaching out and grabbing hold of Dave's dick and stroking it. His eyes lit up as he stared at his hand holding his first hard cock.

"Damn that's big" he said holding his hand tight around Dave's cock and laughing nervously.

"You think that's big, you should see Brian's," Dave said and Todd's focus moved back to me. I blushed and spat out his cock.

I stood up, my sweatpants bowed out dangerously where my impossibly hard cock ached to be set free. I pull the waistband out over my cock and let them fall to the floor.  My dick jumped out and slapped my abs. It hung in the air floating in front of Todd's face mesmerizing him. He reached up and grabbed my cock holding it in his left hand and Dave's in his right comparing them.

"Damn, you're both huge. You put me to shame," he said looking down at his own cock flexing and drooling precum.

"You have a great cock" I said stooping back down and taking it in my mouth again.

"Fuck," Todd said as I took him again to the hilt massaging him with my throat and tongue.

He continued to look closely at Dave's dick exploring it with his hand.

"Damn, I never thought I'd be doing this," Todd said giving another nervous laugh but not letting go. Dave inched closer and closer to Todd face. I shifted between stroking Todd's cock and licking and sucking it, edging him but pulling back as I sensed him getting close. From what Dave had told me, I assumed the moment he came the fun would be over. I wondered what was going through his head but didn't need to speculate long because he leaned in and tentatively licked Dave's cock. Dave nodded to Todd to go ahead and Todd leaned in and slipped Dave into his mouth. I could feel

Todd's cock pulse in my hand at how excited he was to suck his first cock.

Dave told me afterwards that he wasn't very good at it but he gave him an "A" for effort. Dave wasn't about to tell him he didn't give a great blow job, he was a straight boy after all and clearly new to cock sucking so he pretended to enjoy it.

I sensed Todd was getting closer now, his big balls pulled up tight ready to be drained. I couldn't tease him any longer. I grasped his cock by the root and stroked him while I licked and sucked at his sensitive shaft. He suddenly started to erupt inside my mouth filling it with the most bitter cum I'd ever tasted. I still managed to swallow it anyway pondering what made his taste so differently from Dave's.

Dave pulled his dick from Todd's mouth and stroked it violently until he began to shoot volley after volley of warm cum all over his straight teammate's face. Todd just took it wincing a little as the first glob hit him on the cheek. After a few more shots sprayed his face, he seemed to start enjoying it to the point where he actually stuck out his tongue to lick some cum that had run down his face to his lips. I cleaned the last of his acrid cum off his shaft and from his pube stubble before sitting back and standing up.

I'd been stroking myself the whole time and was on the edge as well. I stood in front of Todd and launched my own ropes of cum at his face. He actually opened his mouth this time and caught my seed on his tongue. He kept it open as I launched another spray at him, landing it on his mustached upper lip and across his bared tongue. Some more landed on his face next to his nose and my last glob hit his chin. His face was painted white with our combined cum and he sat there licking his lips and savoring our loads. Maybe he wasn't as straight as I thought, or maybe all guys just enjoy cum when they get a taste for it. Todd even leaned forward and took my softening cock in this mouth for a minute licking off the remaining cum and tracing my big head with his tongue.

Though we were the first cocks he ever sucked I'm guessing we wouldn't be the last from his reaction. I only hoped he improved with practice.

# CHAPTER 14

# DAVE: BRAWL

I couldn't believe I'd gotten to suck Todd's dick, and he'd actually returned the favor. Things got quiet after it was over. I think the events of the evening, starting with Daniella's betrayal, had taken a toll on him.

"You can crash here tonight if you want," I offered as Todd cleaned off his cum-covered face with my towel.

"I should go," he said sadly. I knew his head must have been racing with every possible emotion all at once. I knew mine was the first time with Brian.

"I'll at least walk you down," I said, pulling on my sweats. Brian seemed to sense that I needed a minute alone to talk to Todd and stayed in the room, still naked.

Todd finished getting dressed, and I walked him out into the hallway. It was well after 1am and the hall was quiet.

"You okay?" I asked as we descended the stairs.

"Yeah ... no, hell, I don't know," he finally said.

"It's okay, I felt the same way. It was eye-opening but also confusing," I said.

"Yeah," he said.

"I'm sorry about Daniella. If you need to talk, I'm here," I offered.

"Thanks, I'll be okay," he said. "Listen, can you not tell anyone about this?"

"You know I won't, bro," I said.

"Thank you," he said. At the door, I pulled him into a hug. He was tense at first, then relaxed into my arms as I rubbed his back.

I watched him walk away, hoping I'd not screwed him up or ruined our friendship. I worried that his post-nut clarity would be intense.

As I headed back upstairs, I thought about the that bastard Matty and what our next practice was going to be like. I had no idea how Todd was going to react when he saw him again.

When I got to the locker room for practice the next day, Todd wasn't there.

"He called in sick," Coach said when I asked. I doubted he was actually sick, but I didn't say that to Coach.

When I spotted Matty getting dressed, my fists balled up involuntarily. He didn't seem his blustery self either. He seemed more subdued than usual. After dressing, he left for the pitch without a word to anyone.

Cold rain pelted us all through the first half of practice. It was a miserable practice. We made our way back to the locker room demoralized, sore and soaked to the bone. The whole team seemed to be in the same dismal mood as Matty.

I slammed my locker and walked toward the shower when I spotted Todd heading there too. He was fully clothed, though.

"Why the fuck did you do it!" I heard Todd yell. I raced to the shower to find Todd and Marty wrestling on the floor of the shower. I grabbed Todd and pulled him off Matty, now lying on his back naked, blood pouring from his left nostril.

Todd tried to kick Matty, but I pulled him away. He struggled to break free of my grip as Matty writhed in pain on the tile floor.

"Why the fuck did you sleep with my Daniella?" Todd yelled, pushing against me, trying to get to Matty.

"I didn't know she was your girlfriend. I've never met Daniella," Matty grunted as he tried to stand. The rest of the team gathered around us, watching the drama unfold. Todd stopped pushing against me.

"What the hell is going on in here!" yelled Coach as he stormed into the shower. He surveyed the situation, spotting us, then Matty, who was getting to his feet.

"You, get dressed and take him to the nurse," he said, pointing to Bull who was helping Matty to his feet. "And you two, my office!"

I pulled Todd away from the group and walked him to the office. It had windows that looked out into the locker room with blinds that could be closed for some privacy. Papers littered Coach's desk along with some broken equipment and stacks of boxes around the room.

Todd took a seat, putting his head between his hands. I realized I was still naked and looked around for a towel. I was just about to go out and grab one when Coach came into the door, fuming.

"What the hell was that all about?" He said, looking at Todd. Then he looked over at me, then down at the fact that I was still naked.

"You want to explain?" He asked.

"Todd caught Matty having sex with his girlfriend," I explained.

"Oh, shit," Coach said looking over at Todd with a more sympathetic expression.

"Yeah, Matty said he didn't know she was his girlfriend," I continued.

"How could he not know?" Todd said angrily.

"She never came to any of our games. I've only met her a few times," I said, trying to stay neutral.

"Fuck her! And fuck Matty!" Todd hissed.

"Listen, fighting is a serious matter. I should kick you off the team and report this incident," Coach said, sitting back in his chair and sighing.

"Please ..." Todd pleaded the realization of what he'd done dawning on him as the adrenaline receded.

"I can't have emotions like this dividing the team. You understand?" Coach said. "I'm suspending you for two weeks."

"I understand," Todd said, letting his head droop.

"You can go," he said. I turned to leave. "Can you stay for a moment?" Coach said to me. I turned back, feeling self-conscious being naked and alone in Coach's office. Todd walked past me and let the door close behind him.

"Thank you for intervening. If you hadn't broken things up, it could have been a lot worse," he said. I saw his eyes flick down to my soft cock, then back up.

"He's going to need a friend like you. Can you keep an eye on him?" Coach said.

"Of course, they'll work things out," I said.

"I hope so. You may go," Coach said. I could feel his eyes on my ass as I walked away. I never would have pegged Coach to be into guys. He wasn't all that much older than us, really, maybe ten years or so. He wore a wedding band, so I assumed he was married, but I'd never met his wife or perhaps his husband. He was in incredible shape. He didn't just stand by the sidelines during practice, He ran up and down the field with us, shouting plays. He'd sometimes even jump in the showers with us after an intense practice. He had a lean body where every muscle stood out in sharp definition. Large veins ran up his biceps, and he had a light spattering of hair on his chest.

His dick was average-looking and cut with low-hanging balls. His ass was also tight and round from running and doing tons of squats.

"Thanks for not reporting Todd," I said, turning back. I caught Coach looking at my ass. He shifted in his seat.

"He's a good guy and great soccer player, I'd hate to lose him on the team. He just needs to work on his temper," he said. I felt a tension between us as his eyes went back down to my dick. Without realizing it, I'd grown half hard. "I see why they call you meat," Coach laughed.

I turned beet red and quickly turned and walked back toward the showers, feeling both embarrassed and excited that Coach had commented on my dick.

That evening, I stopped by Todd's to see how he was doing.

"Thank you," Todd said.

"For what?" I asked.

"For not letting me do something I would have regretted," Todd said.

"Sure, don't mention it," I said.

"You believe Matty? That he didn't know it was her?" Todd asked.

"Matty is a lot of things, an ass, a homophobe, a dick at times, but I don't think he would knowingly do that to you. Daniella, on the other hand, is a piece of work. She really did treat you like shit," I said. Matty shook his head.

"I'm coming to realize that," he said.

"We're going to miss having you play next week," I said.

"Yeah, that sucks, but I guess it could have been worse," he said.

We sat in silence for a few minutes. We hadn't talked about what happened the other night. I assumed it was a one-time thing and didn't want to push him. As the silence stretched on, I could feel the tension, like he wanted to say something but didn't have the courage to.

"About the other night," I started. He looked up. "I know it was just some crazy one-time thing, I don't want it to get in the way of our friendship ..." that was what I was going to say, but I was suddenly interrupted mid-sentence by Todd leaning over and kissing me. My eyes opened wide as I opened my mouth to his tongue. It was the last thing I imagined happening. I pushed him back onto his bed and continued to kiss him. He pulled my shirt up my chest, and we only broke our kiss long enough for him to pull it over my head. He buried his face in my thick pelt and licked my nipple.

I could feel his hard dick pressing against mine as we ground our cocks together and kissed. I pulled up his shirt and ran my fingers over the ripples of his abs and hairless torso. His nipples were firm and erect as I flicked them with my tongue.

With one swift motion, I pulled down his shorts, leaving him with his legs in the air, now fully naked on the bed. I dove in and brought his leaking cock to my lips. He grunted in delight as I swirled my tongue over his foreskin. I pulled it up so it just covered the tip, then nibbled on the soft skin.

"Fuck," he said, running his hands through my hair as I deep-throated his cock. His balls tightened, but I wanted it to last, so I stepped back and dropped my sweatpants to the floor. He rolled over and crawled up toward me, ass in the air, and licked my cock. I wet my finger and ran it over his ass crack. While he shaved and trimmed the front, his ass was a wild patch of curly reddish-blond hair. He grunted when I found his pink pucker. I teased his hole while he gobbled down my cock like a pro. He was learning quickly.

"Turn around," I commanded, and he obeyed, shifting around on his bed so he was on all fours, wide-ass facing me.

I got down behind him and pressed my bearded chin into his cleft, rubbing the coarse hair over his hole. He whimpered as my tongue made contact with it. I licked and sucked and flicked my tongue inside him.

"You ever been fucked?" I asked.

"No," he said softly. I could feel his body trembling.

"You act like you want to be," I said.

"It's all I've thought about since I found out you and your roommate have been fucking," he said.

"You want me to fuck your virgin hole?" I said, surprising myself at the commanding character of my voice.

"Fuck yes!" He said, grabbing a handful of each cheek and pulling them apart.

"I've got to warn you, it's going to hurt like hell at first," I told him. In response, he pressed his shoulders to the mattress, pushing his ass out even more.

"If you are sure," I said, hesitating.

"I've wanted that dick, long before Daniella and I broke up. I've wanted it from the first time you joined the team and I saw it in the showers," he admitted.

"You got any lube?" I asked.

"Top drawer," he replied. I found the bottle of lube, then found something else in the drawer. A masturbation sleeve and a dildo. Maybe he's had more practice than I thought.

"I've never tried one. Any good?" I said, holding up the clear plastic sleeve. Todd blushed, realizing what else was in the drawer with it.

"Yeah, not as good as the real thing, but not bad," he said.

"Mind if I?" I asked, turning it over in my hand.

I lubed up my cock and inserted it into the tight, molded pussy. The feeling was a revelation. Had I known things like this existed, I would never have jacked off without one growing up.

I debated bringing out the big purple dildo and getting Todd warmed up with it, but the sleeve had me too close. I wouldn't last long using it. I pulled it off with a wet slurp.

"Roll over," I commanded.

He rolled onto his back. His cock arced up over his abs, looking almost painfully hard.

I slipped the sleeve down over his cock. His eyes rolled back as it gripped him. While he was distracted, I lined my cock up with his tight hole.

"Oh fuck!" He yelped as I shoved into him. I was right. He must have used the dildo already because I slipped in without too much resistance. He'd prepared for something like this? I thought.

I fucked him, looking down at his eyes as they rolled back in his head from overstimulation. I moved the sleeve in time with my strokes inside his ass. He started shaking, and his ass gripped me tight as I saw his load begin to fill the upper part of the sleeve. I pulled it off and watched the spray coat his chest. I was right behind him, filling his ass with my load.

I leaned forward and licked some cum from his chest when I heard a knock at the door.

"Hey, you in there?" Came a voice through the door.

"Shit!" Todd cursed.

"That sounds like Matty," I whispered.

"What should I do?" Todd asked, looking at the door.

## CHAPTER 15

# DAVE: FORGIVENESS

"Can we talk?" There was a pause, and the door rattled like Matty was trying to open it. Thankfully, Todd had the good sense to lock the door before we started. I pulled out of Todd's ass with a loud squelch.

"What was that? I know you're in there," Matty said from the other side of the door. Todd was in a panic to try to pull on some shorts. As soon as he did, my cum began to seep through the material.

"I'll hide in the closet. You talk to him," I whispered, grabbing my clothes and heading to the set of built-in closets along one wall of Todd's room. I quickly shifted some clothes and boxes to one side and got in. It was cramped, but I hoped Todd wouldn't take too long getting rid of Matty.

"What do you want?" I heard Todd say in a clearly annoyed tone.

"Hey, dude, I know you are pissed at me. I'd be pissed at me too," he said.

"You fucked my girlfriend!" Todd said angrily. I was afraid I might have to break them up again, or Todd would really kill Matty this time. I'd have a hard time explaining why I was naked and hiding in Todd's closet, though.

"Listen, I'm sorry about Daniella. I didn't know it was her. She said her name was Stacy," Matty said rapidly, like Todd was about to hit him and he needed to get it all out before the blow came down.

"She did?" Todd said, sounding confused.

"Yeah, dude, I'd never met her before. Honestly, I thought you were making her up," Matty said.

"What's that supposed to mean?" Todd said, getting defensive again.

"Nothing, just ... never mind. It's not important. The point is I didn't know she was your girlfriend. I never would have slept with her if I had," Matty said, ever more quickly than before.

"You really expect me to believe that?" Todd said, simmering.

"I know it sounds crazy, but it's true. I'd never do that to one of my boys," he said.

"That fucking bitch!" Todd said softly.

"Dude, I know. Makes you want to punch a wall or join the other team," Matty said jokingly. The joke didn't cut the tension. Considering that Todd had, in fact, joined the other team just a few minutes ago, it was far too close to home for Todd.

"I'd rather punch the wall," Todd lied. I felt a little hurt, but I understood his not wanting to give Matty any more ammunition for his taunts.

"Yeah, I hear ya. Anyway, I went over to her place just now and told her off. She was pissed," Matty said.

"You did?" Todd said.

"Yeah, she wouldn't let me in, so I told her off through the door with all her housemates watching. I think she was entertaining some other poor bastard," he said. "I stuck around for a bit, and I saw him leave in a huff. She tossed his clothes at him and slammed the door," Matty said.

"That fucking slut!" Todd said angrily.

"Yeah, I knew. I've told all my boys to steer clear of that one," Matty said.

It sounded like Todd had slumped down on the bed.

"So, we cool?" Matty asked tentatively. There was a long pause.

"Yeah, we cool," Todd said.

"You need anything? Maybe an air freshener? Your room smells like ass," Matty said. I heard the sound of skin slapping. "Dude, I'm just kidding, well, not really. Maybe you should get a new roommate. The dude is rank," Matty said.

"Yeah, he is pretty gross. I guess I don't notice it anymore," Todd said.

"I'll let you get back to whatever you were doing before I barged in. See you at practice," Matty said.

"Yeah, see you there," Todd said, and the door could be heard closing and the lock clicking into place. It was none too soon, as my leg was starting to cramp.

"What the fuck?" I said.

"Yeah, I know. That was too fucking close," Todd said.

"Not just that, but about Daniella. She is some piece of work," I said.

"Yeah, I'm so over her," Todd said.

"You might want to change your shorts," I said, pointing to the wet spot spreading up the ass of his sweat shorts.

"Oh fuck! Do you think Matty saw?" He asked.

"Didn't sound like he noticed, except for the smell. Maybe open a window," I said.

"Sorry about that," Todd said sheepishly.

"It's cool. It was your first time. I can't expect you to be perfectly clean back there," I said. It felt weird talking about it, like somehow the details of preparation for anal sex were more taboo than the actual act. I grabbed some wipes from a box by his bed and did some cleanup before putting my shorts back on.

"It was fucking hot," Todd said, smiling as he tried to clean his load from the inside of the masturbatory device he had hastily thrown under his bed.

"It was. I still can't believe that was your first time," I said.

"I can't believe I took this monster," Todd said, grabbing hold of the large mound in the front of my shorts.

"I can't believe it either. You sure you've never been fucked?" I asked.

"Yeah. I've played with my hole before, but I've never taken an actual dick," he admitted.

"I hope I didn't hurt you too much," I said.

"No. Like I said, it felt amazing. I felt so full. I can't describe it," he said.

"So I take it you'd do it again?" I asked.

"In a heartbeat," he said, grinning.

"So you are cool with things?" I asked. I knew I freaked out the first time.

"Yeah. We're cool," he said. He seemed to hesitate, like there was something else he wanted to say.

"I know this is all new to you. It can stay between us if you want," I offered. He let out a breath like he'd been holding it.

"Thanks. I'm still not sure about all this, and I'm not ready for others to know," he said.

"I know, I'm not sure about it myself. Okay if I tell Brian? He's cool, right?" I asked.

"Yeah, that's all right," Todd said. "He doesn't get jealous?"

"Nah, I'm sure he's probably fucking one of our hall mates as we speak," Dave said.

"Fuck really?" Todd asked.

"Yeah, our relationship has been open from the start," I said. It was true. "We went from roommates to lovers to attending several orgies together in less than 48 hours."

"Fuck! You have to tell me all about that!" Todd said.

I told him about our time at camp, and all the guys we fucked together.

"Fuck! That sounds amazing!" He said when I was done. I didn't go into what happened a few weeks ago at homecoming, that was a whole other level. Even I was still processing it.

"You'll have to invite me next time you have an orgy," Todd said grinning.

"I will," I said as I got up to leave.

Todd walked me to the door and surprised me again by pulling me into an embrace and kissing me before I headed out.

## CHAPTER 16

# JUNIOR: LOCKER ROOM SLUT

"You fucked Todd?" I said, staring at Dave in utter disbelief.

"And Matty nearly caught us," he said sheepishly.

"Fuck!" I said.

"You're not upset, are you?" He asked.

"Upset? I'm furious!" I said.

"Really?" He asked. It was unlike me to react like this.

"Yes! You should have invited me to at least watch!" I said, breaking out into a wide grin. He punched my arm.

"Sorry, it all happened so quickly. Then Matty nearly caught us, and I had to hide in his closet," he said.

"He's the one you complained about being so homophobic?" I asked.

"Yeah, he would have gone back and outed us to the whole team," Dave said.

"Does he suspect anything?" I asked.

"I don't think he does," he said. "I don't think he heard us. Besides, I'm not sure I care anymore."

"Really?" I asked.

"Yeah, I'm done pretending. Todd doesn't want anyone to find out about him, but I think I'm ready for people to know," Dave said.

"How do you think people will react?" I asked.

"I'm not sure. I know a few like Matty will freak out, but I think there are a few guys on the team that might be gay or at least curious," he said.

"As long as I get invited to the locker room orgy," I said, with a wide grin.

"I can see you right there in the middle of it, covering in cum," Dave said.

"Fuck, that would be amazing!" I said. In my mind's eye, I could see myself on the floor of the shower room, surrounded by all those hot, naked studs, with Dave in front of me. I could almost feel each hot load hit my skin. My dick twitched as it rose to life in front of me.

"You would love that, wouldn't you?" Dave said, seeing the effect it was having on me.

"You have no idea," I said.

"I think I have some idea," he said, reaching down to grasp my now fully hard and dripping cock.

"You could be the team mascot. We could keep you naked on a leash in the locker room. Anyone could use you any time they needed," Dave said. I was kind of shocked by his dirty talk. This was not the same Dave I started out the term with. The transformation was startling.

He stroked my cock, continuing to whisper what sexy things he and his teammates would do to me.

"Once you are covered in our cum, we would take turns fucking your ass, dumping load after load into your used hole," he said, reaching below my balls and teasing my hole with his thick fingers.

"Oh fuck!" I grunted as it slipped inside me. With one hand, he stroked me while with the other, he began to finger my hole. My head swam with images of big, hairy cocks using my throat and hole. I reached down to pull out Dave's cock.

"No," he said, slapping my hand away. I could see he was hard, but he was content to just stroke me and let me revel in the fantasy he was building for me.

"We won't let you cum until every guy on the team has had his turn. Your hole will be so open and full of cum, it will leak out all over the floor," Dave went on as his fingers dug into my hole.

"What's going on in here?" came the voice of Dave's coach from the shower entrance. All eyes turned to him, looking down at me in my cum-covered state.

"What the fuck! I can't believe you are doing this!" he said.

"We're sorry, coach, but his ass is just so irresistible," Matty chimed in.

"Are we in trouble?" Todd asked.

"Trouble! Of course, you are in trouble!" the coach said. The team backed away, looking down in shame, their cocks still slick with their teammate's cum.

"I can't believe you didn't invite me!" Coach said, pulling his shirt over his head, letting his whistle fall back against his broad, hairy chest. Then he tugged at his shorts and let them drop to the hard concrete floor. His semi-hard dick arched out in front of him. It was thick and long, with a wide head and circumcised shaft. His heavy balls hung low, ready for me to drain.

"You made quite the mess, didn't you," he said as he stepped closer. I could smell his ripe shaft as it came within inches of my face. I stuck out my tongue and lapped up the precum that was already forming. The rest of the team stood around us, transfixed at the sight of their coach's cock slipping into my mouth.

"Fuck, he's got a nice mouth," he said, locking eyes with me. As he ran his hand through my hair, I could feel the hard band of gold around his finger slide along my scalp. He grabbed hold of the back of my head and began to use my throat. Out of the corner of my eye, I could see Dave standing next to Coach, stroking his cock and pinching his hairy nipple. Todd, who had been fucking me when the coach walked in, returned to my ass, and I felt him sink into me with one smooth motion, aided by his teammates' lube.

I moaned as I tried to grip his cock, but my muscles had long since given up protesting. I was open and ready to receive another load. The two of them fucked me from both ends until I felt something warm splatter across my back. I heard grunts from all around me as more loads hit me and began to roll down my sides.

"Oh fuck!" I heard Todd grunt as his hot load filled me and dripped down my balls.

"My turn to try out that sweet ass," said Coach as he pulled out of my mouth and circled around me. I looked up to see Dave looking down at me, wearing a broad smile across his face. Coach spit on my hole, though I didn't really need any more lubricant. The warm spit soothed my aching hole as it trickled down my crack.

I yelped as his cock slammed into me to the root. He was as thick as Dave and nearly as long. He went right to pounding me hard. I felt more hot cum land on my back and in my hair. I looked up to see Matty unloading on my face. I closed my eyes quickly as the hot spray hit me and rolled down my cheek. Just when I thought I'd taken all their loads, I felt another hot spray hit me. It was never-ending. I licked the cum from my lips and felt something just at my tongue's reach. I didn't dare open my eyes but let the cock slip between my lips. I inhaled the scent and knew exactly which dick was in my mouth. Dave's pubes pressed against my nose, and I drew in my breath. My dick jumped as his raw, manly scent filled my nostrils.

I opened my eyes as cum shot from my cock and landed on my cheek. Dave held my shaft by the base and watched me shoot.

"Fuck yeah! You are such a good little slut!" He said. My abs flexed with each pulse I sent soaring. I tasted my cum as it ran over my lips.

Dave leaned in and kissed me, licking the cum from my lips and my cheek.

"Fuck that was hot!" I said. Though no one had actually fucked me, I felt like I was there. It was so hot hearing Dave's deep voice saying all those deliciously dirty things to me. But what really sent me over the edge was Dave himself. I leaned back against his chest, feeling the soft curls of his fur against my back.

He let go of my cock and held his cum-covered hand up in front of me. I instinctively pulled his hand to my face and licked each hairy digit clean. Sucking his fingers was almost as enjoyable as sucking his fat, hairy cock. I felt that cock press into my side and went to shift around so I could return the favor. He stopped me, holding me in place.

"You sure?" I asked.

"Yeah, I'm good. I like to just hold you and make you feel good," he said. With that, he leaned over and kissed me, and we both drifted off to sleep.

## CHAPTER 17

# DAVE: CAUGHT

I wasn't sure what to expect when I went into the locker room for practice a couple of days later. Todd was still suspended, and I knew they had called a truce, but I still thought there might be some awkwardness.

"Hello, faggot," Matty addressed me as I came into the locker room. He used the term like it was a term of affection on me and most of my teammates, but somehow it hit harder this time. I knew he didn't mean anything by it, but it still got under my skin. I guess that was what Matty wanted, to get under your skin. I gripped my fist, resisting the urge to punch him like Todd had.

I had to smile seeing the dark ring forming around his eye where Todd had managed to get in a good punch before I pulled them apart.

"Takes one to know one," I retorted.

"You saying you're a faggot?" Matty said, puffing himself up like he was getting ready for a fight.

I held my tongue for now despite what I had said to Brian. I was still too chicken-shit to come out and say anything. I just walked away.

Matty was the team captain and held a great deal of sway with the team and Coach. If I did say anything, he might try to get me thrown off the team. I loved playing football, I mean soccer, almost as much as I loved fucking. I wasn't about to jeopardize it.

I kept my dick in check, as best I could, and kept my mouth shut. It was a grueling practice, and I ached from muscles I didn't even know I had. My legs were more rubbery than when I fucked Brian. I grabbed my kit and headed out, ready to just fall into bed without dinner when I got back.

I was halfway back to the dorm when I realized I'd left my backpack with my laptop in the locker. I'd come straight from class, so I'd not had a chance to drop it off. I needed to finish my assignments that evening. So no falling straight into bed for me, I guess. I turned around and headed back toward the gym.

It was deserted, my teammates having long since gotten dressed and headed to dinner. I went straight to my locker. That's when I heard the sound of whimpering and moaning. My first thought was that Coach was watching porn in his office and rubbing one out. If he was, I didn't hear the normal, overly exaggerated female screaming that is typical of straight porn. I was reminded of the look he gave me earlier and his comment about my cock. Maybe he was gay, like I suspected? Maybe he was watching gay porn?

I couldn't resist the temptation to sneak up to his office and take a quick peek. It was dark in the locker room. The main lights were out, and I hadn't bothered to turn them on when I'd come in. Only the softer side lights were on, which gave enough illumination to move around but saved energy over keeping the bright overhead lights on when no one was there. There was definitely a glow coming from Coach's office. This meant that if I went up to the window beside his door, I could see in, and he was unlikely to be able to see out if I was careful.

As I approached, the sounds grew louder, and I could make out voices.

"Yeah, you like that dick, don't you?" I heard. It sure sounded like Coach. He was really getting into it, I thought. My curiosity got the better of me. I wanted to see what Coach was packing. I'd seen an impressive bulge in his sweats before, and I'd seen his soft dick in the showers on a few occasions, so I knew it must be above average. I wanted to see what it looked like hard.

"Yes, I love that fat dick, use my hole!" was the response. What I saw next had my mouth nearly hitting the floor. Through the slats in the blinds, I could make out two figures in the office beyond. The first was Coach, his back to the door, completely naked apart from his CrossFits, athletic socks, and his whistle hanging around his neck. His strong, muscular ass was flexing as his legs thrust forward toward the desk. There on the desk, wearing only his jockstrap and his muddy jersey, with his legs up on Coach's shoulders, was Matty.

His face was a mask of pure bliss as Coach railed him so hard the desk looked like it would give way at any moment. I couldn't believe what I was witnessing. Our straight, married coach and our homophobic team captain, in the throes of passion. I found my dick was instantly hard and pushing against my shorts.

"Mmm, fuck I'm so close!" Coach grunted as he continued to pound Matty's hole. I pulled out my cock and began to stroke it, watching Coach's ass tighten with each thrust up inside Matty's guts. I caught up with them quickly, matching Coach's thrusts as if I were pounding Matty.

"Yes, breed me!" Matty purred as he pulled his little cock out of the side of the jockstrap and began to stroke it while Coach slammed into him hard. A sheen of sweat broke out across Coach's back from the exertion as his back muscles flexed. He threw his head back and grunted as he slammed into Matty and held him there. I could make out his balls through his legs flexing as they delivered their load into Matty's guts.

That sent me over the edge. Before I realized it, I was painting the window with my load. Great white streams flowed down the glass as Matty grunted and cum poured onto his belly.

"Fuck that was intense," Matty said as he rested his head on the desk, cum still dripping from his spent cock down his fingers.

I was suddenly aware of just how dangerous my situation was. They would come out to find me holding my dick, leaking great droplets of cum into the concrete floor. I debated trying to clean up my load, but movement inside the office caught my eye.

"Get cleaned up?" Coach said as he pulled out of Matty and helped him to his feet. Coach turned toward the door, slipping off his shoes and socks and grabbing a towel from the rack on the back of the door. For a brief moment before I turned to run, I saw his dick. It was impressive even in its half-hard state. It hung down between his legs and swung back and forth as he took each step. Above his cock was an impressive mound of bush, with a few gray hairs mixed in with the jet-black ones.

I wished I could have stayed and seen that cock up close, but I was out of time. I took off down the corridor and hid in the last row as light from the office spilled into the room. I heard the patter of bare feet on the concrete, then the sound of the shower turning on. I waited a few moments, holding my breath, as I heard another set of feet head in the same direction. I peered around the corner nervously to find the path was clear. I darted past, hoping they weren't looking out the doorway, and headed to the exit.

## CHAPTER 18

# JUNIOR: UNINTENDED CONSEQUENCES

"I knew it! Anyone that is that homophobic is covering for something," I said when Dave returned. He's been out of breath and excited like he was about to burst.

"I know! I just can't believe it," Dave said.

"You should have fucking filmed it, then you'd have something to blackmail him with," I said.

"I didn't think about it, that would be perfect," he said.

"What are you going to do?" I asked.

"I don't know, I like Coach and I don't want to get him in trouble," he said.

"I guess you were right about him too," I said.

"He's got a nice big cock too," he said.

"Fuck! What about Matty?" I asked. Dave held up his pinky. We both laughed, not at the size of his cock, I'd grown to like a little ones like Adam's, but at Matty's attitude. He fit the stereotype of being loud and brash to overcompensate for what he felt he was lacking in that department. But to find out he was a power bottom for Coach was truly the icing on the cake.

"I can't believe I didn't see it sooner. The way he acted on the trip, lying about going out and fucking some rando. I bet he was in Coach's room getting railed all night," he said.

"100%," I agreed.

"Fuck!" Dave said sitting down on his bed.

"What's wrong?" I asked.

"I forgot to get my laptop," he said, "I left it in my locker, that's what I went back for when I caught them.

"They might be gone by now, we could stop by and get it," I suggested.

"I'm too hyped up, I'll just ask for an extension, tell my prof I had computer problems," he said.

"So are you going to confront them?" I asked.

"I don't know, I understand their reasons. Coach is married and Matty, well Matty is Matty," he said rolling his eyes.

"But he says all those homophobic things, he shouldn't be allowed to get away with it," I said getting angrier the more I thought about it.

"I know, it pisses me off too, but he could make life for me even more miserable if he wanted to," he said.

"But you can let on that you know and use it against him," I said.

"If I have to I will, but I don't think you fully understand," he said.

"What's to understand? He's a bigot. And the reason he's such a bigot is he's covering for the fact that he's gay," I said.

"Yeah, but I kinda know where he's coming from," Dave said, looking glum. "I sometimes feel the same impulses. For what my father did to me, I should hate all gays, and maybe I would if I hadn't met you. I can see too much of myself in him and what he is going through," Dave said.

He didn't talk much about his abuse. Dave kept that close to his chest most times. I knew he was serious by the way he brought it up.

"I guess I can see your point," I said, taking his hand in mine.

"You never truly know what someone is going through, what pain they are dealing with," he said thoughtfully.

I put my arm around him.

"You don't think Coach is ..." I started to say.

"Oh God no, it seemed to be consensual," he said sharply.

"Oh, okay," I said.

"No, I just meant you don't know what Matty is going through," Dave said.

"I know, but he's such an asshole," I said. Dave looked out the window for a moment. I often wondered were he went when he got that look.

"I knew this guy back in community college. He joined our basketball games from time to time. He was a lot like Matty, brash, a clown, always getting under people's skin. We weren't close. In fact, I didn't really like the guy. We came back from winter break, and I noticed he wasn't at our games anymore and I hadn't seen him. I thought maybe he had dropped out, so I asked around. I found out he'd killed himself on Christmas Eve." He told me, looking grave. I drew in my breath in shock.

"Fuck, I'm so sorry," I said.

"Yeah, even though I didn't like that guy, it stuck with me, what he must have been going through, the pain no one knew about," Dave said, sitting back against the wall. I hugged him close.

I didn't know what to say. I'd thought about giving up before, nothing more than a thought that passed quickly, but I could understand now why Dave was so reluctant to say anything.

"I'll talk to Matty eventually," Dave said.

"Take your time," I said.

"Sorry to bring down the mood." he said.

"It's ok, you know you can talk to me about anything. Are you ok?" I asked.

"I'm fine," He looked me in the eyes and smiled warmly.

"Okay good," I said holding him close.

"It was hot watching them though," He finally said minutes later.

"I bet it was. Who knows now that you know his secret? Maybe he'd be okay knowing yours," I suggested. He seemed to think for a moment like the thought of doing anything with Matty had never crossed his mind, though Matty had figured heavily into our role play the other day.

"I mean, Coach did seem like he was enjoying Matty's ass a lot," Dave finally said, smiling.

"Not exactly how we pictured it in our fantasy, but I'll take it," I said.

"We'll see. I'm not going to do anything rash," Dave said. Dave rarely did anything rash. He was about the most even-tempered and methodical person I knew. Maybe to a fault. For once, I wanted to see him do something impulsive and throw caution to the wind.

"Do not tell anyone, including Ravi" he said.

"I won't," I said.

"I mean it, no one. If it got out, I'm sure there would be a scandal, and he would lose his job," he said with surprising assertiveness.

"I know, I won't," I said, though I was dying to tell someone.

## CHAPTER 19

# DAVE: COMING OUT

It was good to have Todd back at practice, but it was also a little hard to navigate how to act around him. I tried to act like we hadn't fucked, but in doing so, was I telegraphing exactly that? I also tried not to look at how his cute his butt filled out his shorts as he ran ahead of me down to the field. I couldn't believe that I'd been inside him, that I'd bred that cute tight butt. I have a hard time controlling my dick as it pushed against my jockstrap for the duration of practice.

As we headed into the locker room, I heard Matty laughing and carrying on as usual. He smacked Todd's ass as he walked into the shower room, and I could see Todd trying not to react. I took a shower away from Todd to try to keep from being distracted. Matty took the shower next to me instead.

I saw his jokes and butt smacking in a whole new light now. The image of Coach's dick buried in Matty's hairy ass flashed in front of my eyes, and my dick jumped. I caught Matty glancing down at it.

"Meat must have a hot date tonight!" Matty said, pointing out to everyone within earshot my growing cock. I went to hide it, then something clicked inside my head. Why bother hiding it anymore? I knew what I wanted, and I knew more about myself than I'd known before. Even claiming to be bisexual seemed like a farce at this point.

"That's right, I do have a hot date tonight," I said.

"Bet that thing fucking destroys pussy," Matty said. Behind the taunt, I could sense desire in his voice. From what I had seen in Coach's office, I knew he enjoyed getting railed by a thick cock like mine.

"That's right, it does," I said, holding it up and looking him straight in the eye. "Right now, it wants to destroy your ass!"

He grew bright red. I knew I'd touched a nerve.

At first, there was no reaction from my teammates. Matty's jaw dropped open. The others looked at him, then me, like they were not sure they'd heard me. I felt my body shaking. I felt both incredibly nervous and relieved at the same time. It was out there now. I could still back out and brush it off as a joke if I wanted to.

"Don't get any ideas," Matty said, putting one hand in front of his growing cock and the other over his hairy crack. Now the implication seemed to dawn on the others around the room. The guys looked nervously around, trying not to look at my cock, which they completely failed to do.

"Don't worry, I'm not that hard up for ass. I get plenty of guys with nicer asses than yours," I said, playfully, reaching over to smack Matty's ass. The sound echoed around the shower room. He got a shocked look on his face. The rest of the team began to laugh.

"Fuck you!" Matty said.

"Only if I can fuck you first," I said, holding my hard dick up, pointing in his direction. This too brought a roar of laughter from the others. Matty grew red with anger and embarrassment. It was becoming clear he was getting hard, though he tried to hide it with his hand. He saw me looking down at his dick, jutting straight out about four inches. He turned and stormed off out of the shower.

"Good one!" Fischer, our tall, Germanic-looking goalie, said, beaming ear to ear at me. He turned and went back to getting cleaned up. The banter died out as we finished. I got my dick in check and headed back to my locker. I spotted Matty giving me a cold stare as he slipped on his underwear.

I'd told the truth in there, but it had come out more as a joke than a confession.

"You really gay?" Fischer asked me while I was trying to open my locker with the combination for the fifth time, my hands still trembling.

"Ah..." I stammered.

"It's okay if you are. My kid brother is gay. He came out to me over the summer," he said.

"I guess I am," I said, still not believing I'd come out and said it.

"Cool, I'm glad someone has the balls to stand up to Matty," Fischer said.

"He's just a bully and a homophobe," I said.

"I always say 'a waste is a terrible thing to mind'," he said. I had to giggle.

"Did your brother come out to just you?" I asked.

"He's still in high school. He's too scared to tell our parents which I totally understand. They are super conservative," he said.

"I know how that is. My dad is a fundamentalist missionary and a piece of shit," I spat, surprised at my own venom. I wondered what he would think of me now, coming out like this. He was the biggest abuser and closet case there ever was. I was glad he was no longer a part of my life.

"Yeah, I feel for him; at least they haven't kicked him out yet. I've told him if he needs to get away to some place safe, he can come stay with me," he said.

"I think he'll appreciate that. It's good to know someone has your back," I said, "My uncle took me in when I ran away from home."

"Wow, I didn't know you ran away," he said.

"Yeah, when I turned eighteen, I just left and never looked back," I said.

"Fuck!" he said.

"So it does upset me when I encounter people like him," I said.

"Don't let Matty get to you," he said. "I wouldn't be surprised if Matty was a closet case, the way he acts," he said.

Oh, if you only knew, I thought, shooting a look across the locker room to catch Matty looking in my direction with a nervous look on his face. I wasn't about to out him, but I knew his secret, and it meant I had an ace up my sleeve if he ever fucked with me or Todd. Todd had seemed to melt into the background after my responses in the shower. I looked around and couldn't find him anywhere. I'd have to talk to him later.

"He doesn't bother me, he's harmless. And maybe you are right. I don't fucking care," I said, shrugging.

"Good," Fischer said as he walked past me and to get to his locker. The last thing I wanted to do was make him uncomfortable, so I turned the other way when he dropped his towel.

"Could you do me a favor?", He asked and I turned back toward him. I couldn't help look down at his lean body and long, slender dick. I willed my eyes to stay focused on his face.

"Sure, what is it?" I asked.

"Could you write to my brother?" He asked.

"Uh," I said thinking it would be weird to be writing to a stranger much less someone in high school.

"I just mean let him know it get better," he said.

"Uh sure," I said.

"He doesn't have many role models in our small town and I worry about him,"  he said. I wondered what it  would have been like if I'd had someone reach out to me like that.

"Sure, just introduce us first. I don't want to seem like a creep," I said.

"Okay if I give him your number, he can reach out if he wants to," he said.

"Yeah, that sounds good," I said.

"Thanks!" he said beaming.

I finished getting dressed puzzling on the idea that I could be anyone's role model. I was far to messed up in the head. But if I could help someone I'd want to at least try. I headed out looking to try to catch up with Todd.

"Why did you do that?" Todd said when I caught up with him.

"I don't know. I was just sick of lying," I said.

"You don't think anyone thinks we're, you know," he asked, looking around to see if anyone from the team was around. We were in an outdoor, covered walkway connecting a few of the older buildings. It was nearly deserted.

"No, I don't think anyone suspects that we fucked," I said casually. His eyes grew wide as his head swiveled around in paranoia.

"Relax, it's okay," I added.

"What about Matty? If he finds out, he'll tell everyone," Todd said.

"So?" I said, getting more annoyed at Todd's attitude.

"So! You know who my dad is, right? You know if he ever found out, I'd be disowned, kicked out of school, and who knows what. Fuck!" He said, sitting down in one of the openings that faced the courtyard. He dropped his bag and put his head in his hands.

"Sorry, I didn't know. You'd think in this day and age it wouldn't be a big deal," I said. I found out later that Todd's dad was a conservative senator with a track record of saying the most vile things about gays.

"Maybe to you!" Todd said.

"Listen, I'm sorry. You have nothing to worry about. And besides, I have some dirt on Matty that will keep him from saying one word," I said.

"Really? What?" Todd asked.

"I'd rather not say at the moment, but if it comes to it, just know I have an ace up my sleeve," I said.

"Even still, I think we should cool it for a while," he said.

"OK, whatever you want," I said. I was disappointed, but I had a boyfriend, and I understood he might need some time to sort things out in his own head.

"If you change your mind, you know where to find me. I'll be discreet," I offered. He nodded, but I could tell he just wanted to be left alone.

## CHAPTER 20

# DAVE: ASSISTING COACH

I didn't see Todd until I walked into the locker room for our next practice. He was already dressed and standing at his locker now on the opposite side of the locker room from where I normally had mine. I had a thought that maybe our teammates would catch on to him even more the way he was avoiding me.

I got on my kit and headed out to the field. It was a rough practice. Coach was tougher on us than usual.

"Can I see you in my office for a minute?" Coach asked as I headed off the field, covered in mud and grass.

"Sure, now?" I asked.

"Yes," he said. His tone said it all. He didn't need to tell me what this was about, I knew.

"Whenever you heard is true, I came out to the team. I'm gay," I said, still feeling strange using the term to describe myself.

"Oh, I ... I just ..." he seemed taken aback by my bluntness.

"Most of the guys seem okay with it," I said.

"That's good. I don't want it to interfere with the team," he said. I could feel the tension, and I already knew the source of it.

"Was there anything else?" I asked after a significant pause, in which Coach seemed to be staring at my crotch. The spell was broken, and he looked up.

"Oh, uh, actually, that really wasn't what I was going to talk to you about. I have an opening for an assistant coach. Would you be interested?" Coach asked.

My mind raced. I could see where this might be leading. I looked down at the desk where Matty had been flat on his back getting railed by Coach. I pictured myself in his position. My dick jumped.

"You're one of my best players, and you really know the game. I think you could really go far in coaching," Coach said.

"Let me think about it. I've got a lot going on right now," I said.

"Sure, take your time," he said, seeming just a little disappointed that I didn't immediately jump at the chance. I couldn't tell if he really thought I'd be a good assistant coach or if he had other things in mind. I'd gladly hook up with coach but I didn't want to feel coerced into it. Not that I think Coach would ever take advantage of his position like that. Matty looked like he was enjoying it far to much for there to be anything improper about it, other than such relationships were generally frowned upon by the university.

I was starting to discover the strange divide between out gay men and their closeted counterparts. I could tell he wanted something more but was afraid to take the first step. He was incredibly hot with a nice, fat dick, and I would have done him in an instant, but my life on the team was complicated enough without also fucking Coach.

I headed back to my locker, got undressed, and headed to the showers. Fischer nodded to me as I entered. I spotted Matty as he was leaving, towel wrapped around his waist. He didn't meet my gaze. Todd was nowhere to be found. I closed my eyes and let the water transport me. It washed away the caked mud and sweat. When I opened my eyes, I found I was alone in the shower. I could hear my teammates carrying on over the spray of my single nozzle. Their voices drifted off as they echoed down the corridor and out of the locker room. I was alone now. I enjoyed the quiet for a moment as I let the spray melt my stress away.

"Oh, you're still here," Coach said, seeming startled to find me there. He had a towel wrapped around his waist that fell open, so that now he was holding it in front of him.

"I'm almost done," I said, though I hadn't even soaped up yet.

"You don't mind if I join you?" Coach asked.

"No, not at all," I said, my heart beating faster.

He hung the towel up on a peg and stepped over the lip of the shower. He took a nozzle next to me, though there were plenty of others all around the room to choose from. I looked down to find Coach's cock hanging down in front of him. It looked half hard, with plenty of room to grow from what I recalled. I spotted the wedding ring shining on his finger.

I couldn't help but also react. My dick started to fluff up. I turned away and squirted some soap into my hand, trying to keep my hormones in check. We both showered in awkward silence for a few minutes. Coach spent a considerable time soaping up his cock. I looked down to find he was now nearly hard.

"Mind of their own sometimes, right?" he said with a laugh.

"Yeah," I gulped.

"That's why they call you Meat?" He asked, nodding toward my dick, which was now rock hard.

"I guess so," I said, feeling ridiculously awkward.

"It's a nice one. You should be proud of it," he said. I knew he wanted it. I just wasn't sure I was ready for this to be happening.

"You're not so bad yourself," I found myself saying in a breaking voice. He puffed up with pride and held his cock at the base, showing it off. I grabbed mine and did the same.

"Yours still looks bigger than mine," he said, stepping closer like he was going to lay them on top of each other for comparison, which is exactly what he did. I felt his cock rest on top of mine. He wrapped his hand around both our cocks, holding them together.

"See, no contest," he said, not immediately letting go.

I didn't know what to say or do.

"This okay?" He asked as he began to stroke both of us together.

I nodded my consent. He began to explore my cock, moving his hands up into my matted pubes, then cupped my balls.

"You must cum buckets," he said, hefting each one like he was weighing them in his palm.

"I do. Bet you do too," I said, taking hold of his balls.

"I drain them several times a day, and still, I'm horny," he laughed.

"I know what you mean," I said.

"I bet you are constantly horny. I remember when I was your age," he said.

"You aren't that much older than me," I said. It was true, maybe 10 years older at most. I ran my hands up his body, feeling the ripples of his muscles.

"You must work out a lot," I said.

"It's kinda my job," he laughed. I spotted his gold band, gleaming in the sharp fluorescent light.

"Does she know about your bisexual tendencies?" I asked, nodding at the ring. He seemed embarrassed, looking down at the ring, like he wanted to hide it.

"Sorry, I didn't mean to pry. I honestly don't care. I'm just curious," I continued.

"We don't have much sex anymore. We've been married coming up on 8 years. I don't know if she suspects anything, but if she does, she hasn't confronted me. I think to her it might be a relief that I'm not pressuring her into having sex anymore," he said, looking down at his feet with an expression of something like shame and disappointment.

"Why'd you ever get married in the first place?" I asked.

"It wasn't always like this. When we first met, she was a tiger in bed. Guess people change," he said.

"Did you always feel attracted to guys, or is this something new?" I asked.

"I'd fooled around with guys back in school. I thought it was just a phase," he said.

"Yeah, I thought that too," I said.

"And now?" He said, getting down on his knees, my cock inches from his one mouth.

"I realized I like this way better," I said as he slipped my dick into his mouth. He knew what he was doing. He could take me nearly to the root without gaging.

It suddenly dawned on me that I was getting sucked off by my coach in the open showers where anyone could walk in at any moment. I looked up in a panic to find a figure standing in the doorway. I flinched but recovered quickly when I saw it was Brian.

He must have gotten sick of waiting for me to join him for dinner and came to see what was taking me so long.

His hand was already down his shorts, fondling himself as he watched Coach from behind. Coach had not noticed him and continued to loudly suck my dick.

"Damn, you have a nice dick," he said, pulling me from his mouth to admire my pole, slick with his spit and my precum.

He stood and stroked my dick a few more times with one hand while he took his tool in his hand. He looked up at me, then down at his cock expectantly. I looked past him at Brian, who gave me a thumbs up. He pulled his cock out of his shorts and was now stroking himself furiously.

I knelt down in front of Coach, his dick waving in front of my face. I leaned forward and took it in my mouth, exploring the bumps and ridges of the veiny surface with my tongue. He grabbed my head and shoved it in deep. I wasn't ready for it, so I ended up pushing back and going into a coughing fit. My coughs echoed off the hard tile wall.

Coach looked around self-consciously.

"Oh fuck!" He yelped when he spotted Brian now standing naked only a few feet from us.

"It's okay, he's my boyfriend," I said, smiling.

"Oh," Coach said, still unsure if he should be worried.

Brian came in and knelt down next to me, quickly taking my place. He expertly swallowed Coach to the hilt.

"Oh fuck," he said, his legs shaking with excitement.

I stood beside them, letting my cock slide along Coach's side. I stepped back to watch Coach's ass tighten with each thrust into Brian's mouth. Those muscular cheeks called to me like a siren song.

A patch of light hair ran down the crack, but other than that, they were completely hairless. On each side, a dimple formed as his muscles tightened and relaxed. I stepped closer and pressed my dick along his crack, snaking my hands around his chest to pull him closer.

"I don't know ..." he said when he felt my dick rub along his crack and find his tight hole. "I've never been fucked before," he continued.

"I'll be gentle," I whispered in his ear as I licked the soft lobes. I could see the hair on his neck stand up. I kissed my way down his neck along his spine, tasting the water droplets as I went. I pulled apart those tight globes and dove in.

"Of shit!" He gasped as my tongue lapped around his ring and poked at his opening. I knew he would regret it the moment my girth stretched him to the limit, but I also knew before I was done, he'd be begging me to fuck him harder.

Brian had him distracted enough that he didn't seem to notice when I slipped two, then three, then four fingers inside him. His ass pushed out instinctively as I massaged his prostate. His balls tightened up under him, and Brian stopped sucking him for fear he would shoot his load too soon.

I smacked his ass cleft with my cock, the sound echoing off the hard tiles. Then I pushed my fat head into his hole.

"Oh fuck, you're big!" Coach screamed as I split him open. He squirmed, but I held his hips and waited for his ring to relax. Brian stood and began to make out with Coach, twisting his hard nipples as their tongues wrestled. I sank inside him a few more inches. I felt my pubes tangle with the light strip of hair in his ass and found I was now deep inside him.

He pushed back, and I flexed my dick, expanding inside him.

"Oh fuck!" He whimpered as I began to slowly fuck him. His ass was tight and gripped me as I took small strokes in and out of his inexperienced hole.

"Have you really never been fucked before?" I whispered in his ear.

"Only a few times, but never anyone as big as you," Coach admitted between grunts.

"You like my big dick?" I asked.

"Fuck yes," Coach said as I hit his prostate just the right way. I rested my hand in the middle of his back, and he leaned forward. Brian stood back as Coach bent low in front of him.

"Mmmm," Brian moaned as Coach took his cock in his mouth. I held onto his shoulder and his hip as I picked up the pace. I watched in disbelief as Coach deep-throated Brian's long, fat dick. Where did it all go? I felt the same way when I looked down to see my cock slipping inside his hole.

I was getting close, just the idea that only a few minutes ago my teammates had been all around these showers set me on edge. It wasn't the orgy Brian and I had envisioned, but it was somehow even better.

"Fuck I'm gonna cum!" I yelled.

"Breed me!" Coach responded as he spit out Brian's cock.

Brian got down under Coach and took his cock down his throat. He matched my pace, fucking Coach's ass, and soon he was grunting loudly.

"Oh fuck!" Coach cried as Brian drained his balls. I felt his ass tighten around me. That was all it took. I unloaded deep inside him. I continued to fuck his ass long after my last rope of cum filled his hole. My cum seeped around my shaft and formed a frothy foam as it dripped from him into the wet tiles.

"Fuck!" Coach said as I slipped out of him, and he stood upright once more. Before he could protest, Brian was on him, sinking his cock into his cum-lubed hole. Coach turned toward the shower, letting water run down his back as Brian plowed him hard.

"Oh shit!" Brian cried out as he added his load to mine. Coach gripped the shower head to steady himself. He looked utterly spent.

"Holy shit," he said when he's finally recovered, "that was ...", he seemed to struggle to find an adequate word to describe it.

"Yeah, it was," I said, turning the shower next to him on and rinsing off my dick. Brian came up to me, and we kissed deeply for a moment. I grabbed his dick and felt the slime of both our loads along his shaft.

Coach joined us, and we kissed each other, enjoying the warm water and warmer bodies.

"I'd better get going," Coach finally said. My stomach growled loudly.

"Yeah, we've got to get some dinner. I'm starving," I said.

"It was really nice to finally meet you," Brian said, and Coach gave him a wink. He cautiously looked around the locker room before heading out and grabbing his towel.

I grabbed an extra one for Brian, and we finished drying off quickly, still aware that someone could walk in on us, though it was unlikely.

"You won't tell anyone about this, will you?" Coach asked.

"It will remain between us," I said. "Oh, and if the offer for assistance coach is still open, I'm definitely interested."

"Yes, we can work out the specifics after practice Thursday," he replied. Brian looked at me blankly. "And no, what just happened had or what I'd hoped would happen had nothing to do with my decision to pick you. I meant what I said about you being a great player and making an excellent coach."

"Thanks, I appreciate you saying that" I said then turned to Brian, "I'll tell you about it at dinner."

As we headed out of the locker room, I spotted Matty heading toward it. He saw us and seemed to freeze for a moment, trying to decide how to proceed. I suspected that he was on his way to rendezvous with Coach. I wondered what would have happened if he had been there a few minutes earlier. I saw him veer off in a different direction that I knew only went toward the mechanical building and smiled inside. As we walked past, and I pretended I hadn't seen him.

# CHAPTER 21

# JUNIOR: SIMULATION

"Have you told Amani yet?" I asked Ravi, his mouth was too full of my cock to reply for a moment.

"No, not yet," he said, looking embarrassed.

"You'd better tell her, you don't want to end up like my Dad, married with kids and still sneaking off to suck dick in dark parking lots."

"I know, I should be honest with her, but what if it's a deal breaker for her?" Ravi said, stoking my wet cock.

"If she can't accept you for who you are, then maybe she isn't right for you after all," I said.

"Ugh," Ravi said. His dick had grown soft as his anxiety took over. I bent forward and stuffed his soft cock into my mouth, attempting to revive it and remind him what he would be missing out on.

"Oh fuck," Ravi whimpered, "you need to give her some pointers."

"See, if she knew I could totally show her a few tricks of the trade," I said, smiling. He laughed nervously.

"I just don't know how to begin that kind of conversation," Ravi said.

"Here's what you do," I started, as if I was somehow an expert on the subject, "When you are getting in the mood to have sex, you start to talk about your fantasies. Or talk about some of the craziest things you've ever done sexually. Find out if she has a celebrity crush. Agree with her that whoever it is you think is kinda hot and that you wouldn't mind watching them fuck her."

"Fuck, I like that last one, I know she has a major crush on this one guy she follows on Insta," he said.

"See, bring that up but keep it lighthearted," I said.

"I could give her hints that I'm curious," he said, "like I bet he's hung like a pony."

"Yeah, sure, you can gradually bring things up and see how she reacts," I said.

"Okay, I think I can do this," he said.

"You want to role play it?" I asked.

"Oh, yes!" Ravi said, excitedly.

"Okay, I'll be her, why don't we start by making out?" I said.

Ravi leaned in and started making out with me like I was Amani. He ran his hands down my chest and cupped my pecs like they were breasts. His tongue slipped inside my mouth. It was weird to think that that tongue had been inside her pussy just last night. I cringed at the thought. I had absolutely no desire to go anywhere near pussy. It just reminded me of my mom, ugh. Weird how thoughts of my dad brought me a very different reaction. I dismissed the thought, focusing on how tenderly he kissed me.

He had a different sense about him than usual. Usually, he went right for my cock, but this time he seemed slower and more tender. Maybe there was something to what he said about being more romantically inclined toward women. His soft, deep kisses reminded me of Dave and how he kissed me tenderly like that. I was rock hard, but Ravi ignored my leaking cock.

"You ever think about that guy Robbie on Insta when we're making out," Ravi asked. I slapped him.

"What was that for?" He asked, holding his sore cheek.

"That would be her reaction if you brought it up like that," I said.

"I did what you told me to do," Ravi said.

"No, that wasn't very subtle and sounded too threatening, like you were accusing her of cheating or something," I said.

"Ugh, really? I didn't think it came across that badly," Ravi said.

"Here, let me give it a try," I said.

"Okay," Ravi said as I leaned over and kissed him the way he had been kissing me.

"You are such a great kisser. I love how soft your lips feel," I said. We kissed for a bit more, really getting into it.

"I bet that guy Robbie would be a nice kisser. He's got such full lips. I see how you look at him. I'm not jealous or anything. He's a very sexy guy," I said.

Ravi looked at me, not sure how to react. I went back to kissing him and running my hand down his chest. I cupped his breast and teased up his nipple.

"You're going to think it's silly. Oh, never mind. I shouldn't tell you," I said.

"What?" He asked, trying to get back into character.

"Don't take this the wrong way, never mind. I shouldn't tell you," I said.

"What is it?" Ravi asked.

"Well, I had this dream the other night. It was the strangest thing. I was here with you making out just like we are now," I said. Then I kissed him once more, really going deep this time.

"And?" Ravi said, getting a little impatient.

"Well, we were kissing and all of the sudden you started to shake and your head rolled back and your eyes opened wide. I thought you were having a seizure or something until I looked down to find Robbie eating you out," I said.

"A seizure?" Ravi said, breaking character for a moment.

"Okay, maybe not ... anyway," I said. Then I continued in character again, "I was shocked but also felt kinda turned on. Is that weird?"

"No, it's not weird," Ravi said, trying to act like this whole thing wasn't completely weird.

"Ever since, I've been thinking about it. The three of us doing things together," I said.

"What things?" He asked.

"I don't know, " I said, hiding my face in embarrassment.

"Watching the two of you, and ..." I hesitated.

"And?" He asked.

"And you watching us do things," I said with a nervous laugh.

"What kinds of things?" He asked.

"I found his OnlyFans page. He's got one hell of a cock," I said.

"He does not have an OnlyFans," Ravi said, breaking character.

"I know but a boy can dream. I'm sure there are nudes of him out there somewhere. That bulge is too big for him to not have shown it off to somebody," I said.

"Wouldn't that be something? I find his nudes and show them to her," Ravi said.

"Does she ever watch porn? Have you watched any together? That might be a way to bring it up? Like 'wow look at the size of his cock'" I said.

"No, we've never watched anything like that," He said.

"You should find out if she likes porn and if so, what kinds? Does she have any steamy romance novels on her shelves? You need to do some more research to find out what makes her tick," I said.

"See, this is why I've been hesitant to tell her. I don't know enough about her yet," Ravi said, throwing up his hands in frustration.

"I liked the kissing part. That was nice. You are a great kisser," I said. Ravi looked at me and smiled shyly.

"It's funny that is the first time we've really made out like that. It was kinda hot," he said.

"More than kinda," I said, grabbing my hard cock. He grabbed his own leaking cock. We went back to kissing, this time not playing role-play. I loved the taste of his coconut lip balm and the softness of his lips. I loved the smoothness of his tongue wrapped around mine. I leaned in, pushing him down onto his bed so I was on top of him and our cocks were aligned. I humped his cock, using our precum as lube.

As we made out, I felt his legs wrap around my back, pulling me closer. I rubbed his cock against mine, trapped between my abs and his belly. We both began to moan. Something about the way our bodies were so close had me on edge. I didn't need to fuck him or have him give me a blowjobs. Just the feeling of our bodies pressed together like this was enough to send me over the edge.

"Oh fuck," I heard him mumble into my mouth. Then I felt it, a hot spurt on my abs. His cock pulsed and pressed between us. The sensation sent me over the edge as well. I felt a warm glow envelop us. My balls drained onto this belly and glued us together. We continued to kiss and hold each other as waves of cum poured out of us.

"Fuck that was hot," I said, finally peeling myself off of him, our cum making odd wet patterns in our chest hair.

"I've never done anything like that," Ravi said. He seemed quiet, like he was contemplating something.

"I've tried it before with Dave, but usually it usually just leads to him fucking me," I said.

"Next time we can do that," he said.

"You want to fuck me?" I asked.

"No, I mean you can fuck me, but like what we just did," Ravi said, looking shy and timid, not at all like his normal outgoing and boisterous self.

"I would love that," I said, rolling back over to hold and kiss him again while smearing our combined cum around on his belly.

I was doubtful that Amani would be so open to the idea of Ravi getting fucked by guys, but weirder things had happened. I loved how into it he got and how much he enjoyed giving pleasure. He rarely expected anything in return though I too was happy to do it. I hoped that his girlfriend would be receptive to the idea. It seemed a waste of such natural talent.

"Let me know how things go," I said as I wiped the cum from my chest and licked my fingers.

"I will, thanks for all the advice," he said, lying back on his bed, his spent cock still dripping cum into his hairy brown belly.

I leaned in and licked the last drop from his head, and his abs tightened as he laughed like I was tickling him.

"Fuck, I'd better clean this up before it dries, or I'll have to rip out all my chest hair to get it off me," he said, getting up to get his towel and shower caddy.

"That would not be good, your chest hair is by far my favorite feature of your body," I said.

I was tempted to stay and tell him about what had happened with Dave and his coach, but Dave had sworn me to secrecy.

I knew Ravi wouldn't tell a soul, but I stopped myself anyway. He was right, there was too much at stake.

## CHAPTER 22

# DAVE: BREAKING POINT

"I can't believe Coach gave that faggot the assistant coaching job!" I overheard Matty telling one of his mates on the team. He was looking straight at me with an angry sneer on his face. Overheard wasn't the right word since he was nearly shouting it for anyone on this side of campus to hear. I wanted to wipe that expression off his face with the metal side of the lockers, but I just balled up my fists and took it.

Matty's taunts had gotten worse since he found out Coach had given me the job. It was clear he'd been vying for it. Had I not known Coach better, I would have said getting fucked on his desk was part of the application process. But I knew Matty loved it, and if it would help his prospects, all the better.

"Fuck you," I growled as I pushed past him to get to my locker. He'd taken up residency in Todd's old locker just to make taunting me that much easier. But I saw the way he would catch glimpses of my dick when he didn't think I was looking. I knew he wanted my "Meat" which was probably the real reason he took Todd's locker.

Why are the most homophobic guys the ones that crave cock the most? Brian had told me he'd been blown by way too many conservative fuck heads in the library bathroom to not believe there was something to that theory.

I was getting sick of it. And losing today's match didn't help. We headed back into the locker room drenched in sweat and caked in mud. The mood was somber with none of the usual antics like when we won. Guys just cleaned up, got dressed, and headed out one by one.

"How could you miss that shot!" Matty needled me. The goal was wide open, and I kicked it right into the post, sending it flying out of bounds. That led to the other team scoring the only goal of the game. We fought hard but couldn't get past their defense. I was kicking myself enough, so I sure as hell didn't need Matty rubbing salt in the wound.

"Can we talk?" I asked, standing in the open door to Coach's office.

"Sure, come on in," Coach said. He got up and closed the door behind me after checking that everyone else had left. "If this is about the other day, I know I got carried away. We can keep things strictly professional from now on."

"It's nothing to do with the other day. In fact, that was incredibly hot," I said, feeling my dick harden in my sweats. I wanted to throw him down on the desk and plow his hole again right now, but I didn't want to get distracted from what was bothering me. Should I just come out and tell him I knew he was having sex with Matty as well?

"It was," Coach smiled, adjusting a growing lump in his khakis. "But I get the sense there is something else?"

"Yes, it's about Matty," I said.

"Oh," Coach said, blushing slightly.

"He's got to cool it with the homophobic language," I said.

"I know he's mouthy and a bit of a hothead. It's the main reason I didn't pick him for the assistant coach position," he said.

"I think he's pissed off that you picked me instead," I told him.

"You're probably right. I'll have a talk with him," he said.

I hesitated. I was still unsure if I should bring up what else might be driving Matty to do what he did. Namely, jealousy.

"Was there anything more you wanted?" Coach asked, his hand pressing against his khakis. I found my mouth was parched.

"There is something else. I'm not sure how to tell you this," I started.

"You can be completely honest with me," he said.

"I know about you and Matty," I came right out with it.

"What?" Coach said, his face reddening.

"I left something in my locker the other night. When I came back for it, I heard you two in here," I said.

"Oh shit," Coach said, looking gravely up at me.

"You know your secret is safe with me. I wouldn't out either of you. It's just I feel like Matty might be feeling jealous in addition to not getting the coaching job," I said.

"He doesn't know what we did, does he?" Coach asked.

"No, I don't think he does, but I think he might suspect something," I said.

"Hmm," Coach said, looking past me like he was thinking intently about something.

"I think I know what to do," Coach finally said. "Can you come back in an hour?"

"I have plans with Brian," I said.

"Bring him along," he said with a wide grin on his face.

"Oh," I said, now the gears turning in my head. "See you later than."

"Oh, and thanks again for keeping this all discrete," Coach said.

"Of course," I said, reluctantly turning to leave the office. My dick was hard and pressing into my gray sweatpants. It would be obvious to anyone I ran into that I was hard. I tried to tamp it down as best I could as I headed out of the athletic building to meet Brian.

## CHAPTER 23

# JUNIOR: TEAM MEETING

I spotted Dave coming across the quad toward the little café where I was sitting waiting for him. Even from this distance, I could see his fat cock swinging heavily between his legs in those gray sweats I love so much.

"Hey, sorry I'm late," he said as he sat down at the table.

"You didn't meet with the coach without me, did you?" I said, looking down at the rim of his cock head, clearly visible in the material. Was that a faint precum stain just to the left of it?

"I did meet with Coach, but no, nothing happened," he said.

"Something's got you excited," I said.

Dave looked down at his crotch, then around at the other students dotted around the café. He covered his cock with his hand, looking a little red in the face.

"We have to eat fast. Coach wants us to meet him in about 50 minutes," he said, checking his watch.

"Oh?" I said, now also feeling my cock thicken in my jeans.

"I'm not sure, but I believe we might be joined by someone else," he said.

"Ooh, now I am intrigued," I said. "Is it Todd?"

"No," he said. I noticed that he had not talked much about Todd lately. After they fucked, it seemed like things cooled off between them. I wanted to ask what happened, but sometimes Dave was not very forthcoming with his feelings.

"Okay, I'll let it be a surprise. I hope it is that tall Nordic-looking guy, fuck he is hot," I said.

"Who? Fischer?" He asked.

"I don't think you ever introduced us," I said.

"With good reason, he's straight," he said.

"Since when has that stopped me?" I said.

"No, seriously, he's a cool guy, but I don't get the sense that he's into doing anything," he said.

"Pity, does he have a big dick? He exudes big dick energy," I said.

Dave blushed.

"Fuck, I wish I was on the team," I said.

"As our mascot," he said.

"As the team's toy, they can all use me however they want," I said, "except Matty, he sounds like a prick."

Dave reddened again.

"It's not Matty, is it? Who will be joining us?" I asked.

"I think our order is ready," Dave said, getting up to retrieve our plates and escaping my interrogation. Fuck, really?

I let the subject drop. I'd know soon enough anyway. We wolfed down our food and got up to leave. We had ten minutes to spare to head back to the athletic building.

"What's Todd doing here?" I asked, spotting him going into the building ahead of us.

"I don't know?" Dave said, looking confused.

The lights were set on the nighttime setting, so the halls were dimly lit until you set off the motion sensors. Dave got out his key to open the locker room door but found it was already unlocked.

Only a few lights were on inside, lending an eerie glow to the echoing space. It was the perfect setting for some slasher horror film.

"What the fuck is going on?" Todd said, spotting us come in.

"Did Coach ask you to come too?" Dave asked.

"Yeah, he told me there was something he had to discuss with me," Todd said.

We walked to the office and found it was dark and empty.

"I heard the shower going," I said.

"What the fuck!" Todd gasped when we reached the opening to the shower.

Inside, we could see Coach from behind, fully naked, his muscular gluts flexing as he thrust his hips forward. In front of him stood Matty, also naked, holding onto the shower nozzle, pushing his ass out to take a raw pounding from Coach.

"Oh shit!" Matty yelped when he heard Todd's gasp over the din of the shower. He jumped away from Coach, his hard little cock bouncing up and down with each step. He looked like a wild animal caught in a trap. His eyes were wide and his mouth gaping open.

Coach turned to spot us, his huge cock jutting up and to the left pulsing with his heartbeat.

Matty was beet red and attempting to hide his hard dick and pretend like we hadn't just caught him getting railed by Coach.

"You ..." Todd stammered, anger boiling up in him.

"This is the dirt I had on Matty. I didn't tell you about it the other day," Dave said.

"All those horrible things you say," Todd spat.

"I ... I ..." Matty tried to speak but it came out more like the croaking of a frog.

"I invited them," Coach said.

"What the fuck? Why?" Matty finally found his words.

"To resolve this conflict once and for all. I can't have this feud ruining our chances of making it to the finals," Coach said.

"But," Matty started.

"You fucked Todd's girl. Now it's time he gets to pay you back for that," Coach said.

"And I've heard you've been taunting Dave ever since he came out to the team. You owe him and his boyfriend an apology as well," Coach said forcefully.

"But Coach," Matty said, looking down at the tiled floor in embarrassment and humiliation.

"Well? You gonna just stand there or are you going to come in here and join me?" Coach asked.

Todd looked at Dave in shock. Dave mouthed something like, "I didn't tell him anything."

"He didn't tell me, but it was painfully obvious the two of you fucked," Coach said, seeming to read their minds.

These three hot studs standing here and Matty cowering in the corner were too much for me. I stripped off my shirt and unbuttoned my jeans while kicking off my shoes. Dave looked over at me stripping and shrugged his shoulders. He too began to strip off his shirt.

Todd hesitated, looking at Coach and then Matty. He looked back at Dave, who had just dropped his sweats. He was naturally not wearing anything under them. His dick swung out in front of him, already leaking and semi-hard.

I stepped toward Todd and took hold of his shirt. He looked at me, then lifted his arms to let me pull it over his head. His skin twitched where my fingers grazed his soft, alabaster skin, touched with blond hairs.

I got down on my knees and looked up at him. He looked down at my naked form, my hard cock pointing up toward my belly button. I could see the growing lump in his athletic pants and pulled down the waistband. He was wearing a bright blue jockstrap. His cock was pushing the material out, so you could see his hairless crotch and smooth balls if you looked in the side. I pulled the waistband down, freeing Todd's cock from its prison. It swung up and hovered in front of him.

I leaned forward and licked the wetness from his piss slit, tasting the salty sweetness of his precum. Todd grunted as I took him down my throat, swallowing him to the point where I could lick his smooth, tight balls. Todd wasn't as big as Dave, so I had no problem swallowing him without gaging.

"That's right, Meat, go ahead and use his ass," I heard Coach say. I was so lost in sucking Todd's cock, I hadn't noticed that Dave was no longer standing next to us. I dislodged Todd's cock from my throat, lapping up a squirt of precum before turning to see what Dave was up to.

## CHAPTER 24

# DAVE: PAYBACK

Brian seemed preoccupied with Todd's dick jammed down his throat, so I stepped out of my sweats and headed into the shower. First, I stepped right up to Coach and grabbed the back of his head, pulling him into a deep kiss. I knew Matty was watching. I wanted him to see us. I imagined his jealousy building as he watched me grab Coach's dick, lined it up with mine and stroked them as one. I couldn't get my hand around both of them. For a moment, I pictured our dicks pushing into Matty's hole, splitting him in two.

"That's right, Meat, go ahead and use his ass," Coach said as I stepped over to Matty standing in the corner of the shower room facing me. He gave no resistance as I twisted him around so his gaping hole was on display in the strip of hair running down his crack.

Coach stood beside me holding Matty in place as I lined up my dick with his already open and ready hole.

"You want this cock, faggot?!" I growled and slapped my girth across his right ass cheek.

Matty reluctantly nodded.

"Say it, faggot, say you want me to breed your hole," I demanded.

"Breed my hole," Matty said quietly so it was barely audible over the sound of the water hitting the hard tile.

"I didn't hear that, what did you say?" I demanded.

"Please breed me," Matty pleaded more loudly this time.

"I like the 'please'. You may call me 'sir'," I said in my gruffest and most masculine tone.

"Please fuck me and breed my hole, sir," Matty said looking like a puppy that had peed on the rug.

"And after that, you will take a load from each one of us," I said.

"Yes, sir," he said pushing out his ass. Like Brian, I wondered if he too must have fantasized about getting a load from each of his teammates.

"And you will stop with the homophobic slurs, or I'll fuck you like this in front of the entire team," I said.

"Yes, sir," he said, though I wondered if he really wouldn't mind that kind of humiliation. I realized he wanted to be humiliated and dominated. He acted that way to get people to stand up to him to take him down like I was doing now. He must revel in it.

"Oh fuck!" Matty cried out as I shoved the full length and breadth of my dick up inside his guts without warning. I looked up to find Todd standing next to me, stroking his dick as he watched me plow Matty's hole.

To my left, I saw Brian was down in his knees, bobbing his head up and down Coach's pole. Coach had his eyes closed, focused on the magic Brian was performing in his dick.

Matty felt warm, wet, and wide open from Coach's preparations. He offered no resistance as I pulled nearly out of him and slammed back in hard. I was a little disappointed that I wasn't hurting him more. I wanted to teach him a lesson, but even my dick wasn't enough on its  own.

I continued to fuck him, watching my cock disappear into his hairy hole. I felt Todd press up against me. I turned my head, and he kissed me, slipping his tongue into my mouth. His dick pressed into my side as we made out while I continued to slam into Matty. Matty began to whimper, and I felt his ass tighten around me. I reached under him to feel his big balls pulled up against him and his cock beginning to shoot a load into the shower wall and tiled floor. He'd not touched himself. His hands were holding himself up against the wall. His teeth were gritted tight as I pounded a load out of him. His ass muscles fluttered, milking my dick.

"You must have really wanted my Meat to cum hands free like that," I growled in his ear.

"Fuck yes!" He replied.

"Fuck yes, sir," I corrected him, slapping his ass so hard a red palm print rose on his pale skin.

"Yes, sir," he whimpered.

"You ready for my load, faggot!" I said. It wasn't a question.

"Yes, sir, give me your cum," he whimpered as he continued to leak the last drops of cum from his piss slit.

I slammed into him one last time, depositing the first load of the evening deep inside him. My body shuddered as my balls drained. My legs nearly gave way as I held him, impaled on my cock.

Brian and Coach were watching as I slowly pulled out, leaving a trail of white seeping from his messy hole, coating his hairy balls.

Todd wasted no time pushing my cum back into Matty. He pressed his dick deep into Matty's used hole with such force that it knocked him into the wall, where he banged his head against the hard tile. Matty didn't complain, though. He took the pain in stride. I felt like I needed to humiliate him just a bit more.

"Clean up my cock," I said, standing beside him and holding it up toward his face. I took hold of his head and moved him lower. He put up some resistance this time, knowing where my dick had just been.

"Do it, clean it up, faggot," I said, pushing his head down until my slimy dick was pressed into his cheek. Matty reluctantly began to lick my pole clean and slipped it into his mouth. His mouth felt almost as good as his ass. It was clear he'd sucked plenty of big dicks before, because I didn't feel any teeth, only his warm tongue and throat.

The action of his tongue kept my dick hard and got me close to cumming again. I watched Todd's dick slam into Matty's ass so fast that I thought the friction might singe his ass hair.

"Oh shit!" Todd grunted as he added his load to mine, deep inside Matty. I could see his dick expand each time he shot another stream into him.

Todd pulled out and leaned against the wall for a moment, catching his breath.

"Come over here and make him clean you up," I told Todd as I pulled my dick from his throat.

Todd still seemed wobbly, so I let him lean back against me as Matty, resigned to his punishment, lapped at Todd's cock.

"I'll go last. I love sloppy fourths," Brian said, gesturing for Coach to go next.

Coach stepped up behind Matty and set his fat cock in the cleft of his ass. Cum seeped out of his hole onto the tip of his cock.

"You are so open and wet, I can barely feel my dick go inside," Coach said. Matty tried to flex his ass and tighten around Coach, but his sphincter muscles were exhausted. Coach pushed forward and slipped inside easily. His big dick displaced so much cum that it began to leak out, in a stream into the floor.

Coach showed no mercy and drilled Matty for all he was worth. I was sure he'd have a hard time sitting down for weeks afterwards. Coach knew how to fuck. His whole body seemed to get into the motion. I could see each set of muscles tighten and relax with his thrusts. His ass looked especially inviting as the dimples formed when he pushed in.

I stepped up behind Coach and let my dick rest in his crack as he pounded Matty. I was hard again from Matty's licking and needed to get it wet again. I pushed in, prying Coach open.

"Fuck!" Coach said, pushing back and waiting a moment as I got inside of him. "I'm normally a top, but damn if you aren't going to make me into a bottom."

"You have too good an ass to waste only topping," I said.

I held on and let him set the pace, sinking into Matty as I pulled out, then pushing back on my dick as he pulled out of Matty. Soon he was grunting and panting, ready to fill Matty with another load.

I felt his ass tighten around me and shoved forward as he filled Matty with even more cum. Coach fell against him, wrapping his arms around him as the three of us connected through our dicks pressed against the wall. I wasn't ready to cum again, but I still enjoyed feeling the waves of pleasure Coach was feeling as his balls drained. I felt a vibration under me and realized Matty's legs were shaking. He was having a hard time standing.

I pulled out of Coach and stood back, watching as Matty's dick shot a second load under him this time into Brian's mouth. I hadn't seen him duck under him, but there he was, draining Matty's balls. As Coach pulled out, a gusher of cum leaked out with him as his balls tightened and bounced with each jet of cum he delivered to Brian.

"I've got to sit down," Matty said, slumping against the wall on his way to the floor.

"You've got one more load to take," I said, impatiently.

"Give me a minute, please sir," Matty pleaded. Sitting on the floor, his still-leaking dick resting in his thigh. He brought his legs up and traced the lip of his overstretched hole.

"While you're down there, you can clean him up," I said, nodding at Coach's cum-covered cock.

Matty looked up at it and licked his lips. For all his reluctance to do it at first, he now seemed eager. Coach stood over him, leaning at an angle, and fed him what was now the cum from all three of us.

Just watching him feverishly lick Coach's dick made my dick jump. I was building toward a second load soon.

## CHAPTER 25

# JUNIOR: DOUBLE TEAMED

I watched as Dave plowed Coach's ass while he fucked Matty's used hole. I saw Matty's balls tightening. He'd already shot his load once hands-free, and now it looked like he was building toward a second load. I looked down at the mess of cum on the floor, feeling like that would be a waist and squatted down beneath him. The tile was slippery with still-warm cum. I looked up at Matty's hairy chest above me, and his short chubby dick leaking a line of precum that nearly stretched to the floor. I opened my mouth and held out my tongue, tracing the bead to its source.

I don't think Matty was even aware of the fact that I was under him. His eyes were closed tight, and his jaw locked in place. Was he in more pain than we thought? I almost pitied him, but I remembered the things Dave had told me he'd said. His legs were shaking, and I realized the pain may not be in his ass but a leg cramp forming.

I heard Coach grunt and saw his balls tighten as they slapped Matty's. He slammed inside hard, and I could see his perineum throb as he began to unload inside Matty. I leaned forward and took Matty's cock in my mouth. He must have been already close because I had barely gotten it in my mouth when I felt a hot jet hit the back of my throat.

I shouldn't have been surprised by the sheer volume of cum pouring from those big swollen balls of his. I swallowed and swallowed, but it just kept coming. I could feel Matty's whole body shaking as his muscles tensed. I was afraid he might collapse on top of me.

I let his cock slip from my mouth, still dribbling cum onto my chin. Dave was looking down at me with a grin on his face. He knew how much I loved cum, especially his. I moved out from under Matty, and he tried to stand, then not able to manage it, slid down the wall. Cum was leaking from his hairy ass hole as he leaned back and caught his breath.

I watched him play with the loads spilling out of him. It was my turn to fill that gaping hole. Matty weakly protested. Then the idea hit me.

I rolled onto my back, feeling the sticky cum on my skin. I pulled my cock away from my belly and held it up for Matty to see.

"You were a champ at taking some really big dicks just now, but are you up for a real challenge?" I asked.

"Huh?" Matty looked over at me, his head cocked to one side.

"I'm sure you can take me easily now that they have already opened you up, but what about two of us?" I said, nodding over at Dave, who was still hard and ready to shoot again.

"Oh no, I don't think I could," Matty said, pulling his legs up to his chest, a genuine look of fear on his face.

"I bet you could do it, especially now that you are so open and lubed up," I said, moving toward him. I reached my hand down into his hole. Four fingers and my thumb slipped easily inside him. I pushed up to my knuckle and still felt only the slightest resistance.

"See," I said, holding up my cum soaked hand as exhibit A.

"I've never done anything like that," Matty whimpered.

"But you've been curious," I said.

"Is it even possible?" Matty asked, now looking more intrigued than fearful.

"I've seen it done," I said, recalling watching my dad and Colin fuck Timmy. That seemed like a lifetime ago, though it had only been two months.

"Bullshit," Matty said.

"I have, and not just in porn. It was at a friend's place this summer," I said.

"Fuck!" Todd said.

"I'll have to tell you about it later," I said.

"Come on, are we doing this or what?" Dave said impatiently.

"Do I have a choice?" Matty asked. Not really asking, he knew it was inevitable.

"You always have a choice, but if you don't, there will be other consequences," Dave said. I wondered what those might be.

"Let's get this over with," Matty said, with a tone of reservation hiding an undertone of excitement. "What do I do?"

"Get on top of me and ride me," I said.

"That is going to kill my knees," Matty said.

"Wait a sec," Coach said, turning and leaving the shower. He returned a moment later holding a practice mat, like they use for wrestling.

I flopped down on my back atop it. Cum smearing across the surface.

"Don't worry, it's washable. I'll just hose it down after," Coach said.

Matty got up on top of me with his fat thighs on either side of me. His limp cock rested on his balls as he lowered himself onto my cock. I slid in easily. His expression softened as he felt me throb inside him. It was clear he was enjoying this more than he was letting on. Dave knew what to do, from the stories I'd told him about my dad and Timmy.

I was starting to worry though. Timmy was used to having a man's arm up inside him, so two cocks was a piece of cake. Matty had presumably only had dicks as big as Dave's and now mine inside him.

Dave knelt down behind Matty, reaching his arms around him and holding him for a moment. There was tenderness there like there always was with Dave. He could certainly fuck, but I think to him there had to be a component of love to it for him to get into it.

"Ready," I heard him whisper in Matty's ear.

"As I'll ever be, sir" Matty said, bracing himself.

I looked up to find Todd and Coach towering over us, stroking themselves as they watched.

Then I felt the tip of Dave's cock press against mine and slowly move forward.

"Oh fuck, I don't think ..." Matty bellowed. I felt him try to clamp down on us with what little strength was left in his sphincter. Dave hugged him to his broad chest and kissed his shoulder.

"You're doing fine," he whispered to him softly. Matty seemed to melt in Dave's arm. Maybe the tension between them had been leading to a moment like this. Though Dave had been play-acting the tough, dominant guy, he was really a teddy bear at heart.

I felt Dave slip in a little deeper as Matty relaxed. I could see Matty gritting his teeth. He leaned forward, holding himself a few inches over me. His weight could easily crush me, but he did his best to hold himself up.

I felt Dave's balls come into contact with mine.

"See, you did it," Dave said.

Matty reached back in disbelief. His fingers traced where both of our cocks disappeared into his hole.

"Fuck! I've never felt so full," he said.

I could tell it was taking all of Dave's resolve to hold back, but he waited, letting Matty get used to the feeling of two big dicks splitting him open.

I felt Dave begin to retreat, his cum-lubed cock sliding along my shaft. This is what my dad must have felt when Colin was fucking Timmy. The feeling was overwhelming. I knew if I wasn't careful, I would explode prematurely. I bit my lip to try to distract myself, but everything was triggering me. When I looked up, I saw Todd reaching for Coach's dick, and Coach in turn took hold of his. They were stroking each other, watching us.

"Oh shit," Matty grunted in relief as Dave's cock slipped out. Dave didn't let him enjoy the relief for long, though. I felt his cock slip back alongside mine once more. Matty cringed and sucked in a deep breath, trying to block out the pain. Dave waited a moment, then pushed forward, taking small strokes. Matty's expression was somewhere between agony and delight as Dave and I pressed against his prostate.

Matty's cock grew hard and began to leak onto my belly. With each thrust, Dave pushed Matty into me, rubbing his cock over my abs, leaving a wet residue behind. Dave began to pound Matty harder now. I loved the feeling of his cock sliding against mine, lubed by three loads of cum.

"Oh fuck!" I cried. I couldn't hold back any longer, the feeling was just too intense. I added my load to Matty's ass. I felt hot, wet drops hit my chest, and at first, I thought it was coming from Todd and Coach. Then I looked down and saw Matty was cumming for a third time. It wasn't as forceful as the first two times, but it was still an impressive pool gathering on my belly. Then I did feel something start to rain down on me. I looked up to catch Todd launching a stripe of cum at my chest. Coach was gripping the base of his cock as his body shook, and volley after volley of cum shot out, landing on Matty and me.

My cock was super sensitive, but I was pinned down by Dave and Marty, so I wasn't going anywhere. Dave's forehead crinkled up, a sure sign he was ready to blow.

"Fuck!" He grunted as he plowed a second load into Matty. His body shuddered, and I felt warm, wetness all around my cock. I could feel his cock expand and press into mine, and the hot jet across my sensitive skin. Matty collapsed on top of me, nearly knocking the wind out of me. I was surprised, though, how much I enjoyed being smothered by the big, hairy oaf.

I turned my head to the side to catch Todd now on his knees, sucking a load from Coach. Coach grabbed the back of his head, his big hands running through Todd's silky blond hair.

"Mmm," Todd hummed as Coach drained whatever was left in his balls down Todd's throat. Coach held his head in place with Todd glued to the base of his cock until Todd pushed away, gasping for air and coughing up globs of cum.

"Fuck!" I gasped as Dave pulled out, leaving me still inside Matty. I felt a cum lava flow running down my shaft and balls. I couldn't believe what we'd just done. It was like something out of a perfect dream. I didn't want to wake up.

Finally, Matty rolled off of me onto the mat. Both of us and the mat were smeared with cum.

Dave fell to my other side, his thick, muscular arm draped across my chest. I almost drifted off when I felt warm water spraying me.

"Time to clean up and get the hell out of here. The cleaning crew will be here soon, and we don't want them to find us like this," Coach said holding up a hose with a sprayer nozzle attached to the end.

"You could have warned us," I said, getting up, dripping wet.

"It was his idea," Coach said, playfully turning the spray on Todd. Todd jumped out of the way, and Dave leaped up to grab the sprayer. He turned it on Coach. We laughed, and then Coach once more reminded us we should hurry. Matty stumbled to his feet reluctantly, as Dave hosed down him and the mat. I watched with some sadness as the cum circled the drain and disappeared.

## CHAPTER 26

# JUNIOR: LUCKY FIND

"You guys had another orgy and didn't invite me? I'm going to start taking this personally," Ravi said when I told him about what happened the night before. I left off the fact the Coach was also there because we were all sworn to secrecy by Coach before we left. We were just in time leaving too. The cleaning crew was just arriving as we stacked the mat against the wall to dry before leaving.

"I didn't know it was going to be an orgy. All Dave told me was that we were supposed to go to the gym in an hour," I said.

"And there you found Todd and Matty?" He asked.

"Yes, turns out Matty is an insatiable bottom. He took all of us and Dave and I both fucked him at the same time," I told him excitedly.

"Fuck! I can't believe I missed that, you could have at least filmed it," Ravi said.

"If that ever got out there would be a huge scandal for sure," I said.

"Don't worry I won't tell anyone," Ravi said.

"I wasn't supposed to tell you at all, but I know you won't tell anyone," I said.

"He took both of you?" Ravi asked looking like he was trying to calculate the circumference of our combined cocks and the displacement volume of our combined cum. For all I knew that might have been exactly what he was thinking. Of course his calculations would be missing an additional load from Coach.

"It was a tight fit but he was a champ," I told him.

"You are so fucking lucky," he said.

"So what was it you wanted to tell me? Hopefully something good," I said.

"Oh it is, I told her," Ravi said grinning from ear to ear.

"It went ok then?" I asked.

"Better than ok, she was super into it," he said.

"Oh shit, you have to tell me how it went down," I said.

"Ok so, we were hanging out at her place, her roommates were out ..." he began.

We were both on our phones when I glanced over and saw her liking a post from that guy.

"That's I hot picture, I wish I had his body," I said.

"He is hot but I bet he he's terrible in bed or has a tiny penis, he's too perfect," she said.

"No he's definitely packing, didn't you see that leaked video," I said.

"No, there is a porn video of him?" She asked.

"Sure, let me find it," I said. Pulled up the video. Some ex of his had posted it and though an attempt had been made to clean up the damage I was able to find it in one of the darker corners of the web.

"See here it is," I said holding up the phone already playing his jerk off video. I'd in fact jerked off to it several times already since finding it. I was hard now watching it again now with her there.

"Wow, ok I guess I was wrong," she said.

"Not the biggest I've ever seen but respectable," I said.

"You've seen bigger?" She asked.

"Well sure, I watch all kinds of porn," I told her not sure I was ready to tell her the biggest one I'd seen was in person and had been in my throat and ass.

"You're not weirded out seeing another dude's dick or him jacking off like that?" She asked.

"I'm pretty open minded," I said. I was trembling. It was going better than I thought but I didn't want to reveal too much too quickly.

"You ever been with a guy," she asked point blank. I was stunned, I wasn't sure what to say. It seemed too soon. I'd prepared for this but having her ask me like that sent me reeling.

"Oh shit you have?" She said reading my expression more than anything. I nodded.

"Fuck that's kinda hot," she said.

"Really?" I asked.

"Sure, there is something super naughty about it," she said with a mischievous grin on her face. God I love this woman. I'm going to marry her one day, I thought.

"It doesn't freak you out?" I asked.

"No, should it?" She asked.

"No, I guess not, I was just so nervous you would think I'm a weirdo," I said.

"I think you are a weirdo anyway, this doesn't change that at all," she said playfully. I giggled.

"So come on, tell me what you've done," she asked.

"You really want to know?" I asked.

"I want all the gory details," she said. She reached down and pawed at the lump in my sweats.

"Ok, well, my first night on campus I had one of my hall mates blow me," I told her.

"Oh really? Let me guess which one. Have I met him?" She asked. I nodded. "It's that cute guy around the corner from you right? What's his name, Ryan?"

"Brian, yes it was him, we've actually been having sex on and off ever since," I told her.

"Fuck!" She said. My heart skipped a beat, was that too far? Did she think I was cheating on her?

"If this is serious I can stop," I said looking at her gravely.

"No, I was picturing the two of you, bet he has a huge cock and fucks you with it," she said grinning.

"How did you know?," I asked.

"Who can resist that big brown ass," she said. I leaned to the side and she pulled down my sweats to smack my ass.

"She's got you there," I said, interrupting Ravi's story.

"I told her all about you and your escapades, and how you sucked me off the first night we met," he said.

"Wow, and she took it all in stride?" I asked.

"We fucked like rabbits all night long she was so horny," he said. I tried to picture Ravi fucking her and just couldn't picture it. I liked my image of his big hairy ass taking my cock so much better. But it is who he is and I can't argue with that.

"So now that she knows do we have to stop fucking?" I asked worried that one of the best asses I've fucked on a regular basis would now be off limits.

"Oh god no!" Ravi said to my great relief, "she just has one stipulation."

Here it comes, I thought steadying myself.

"She wants to watch," Ravi said almost giddy with excitement.

"I don't know ..." I said seeming to pour icy water over his exuberance.

"She doesn't want to join in, in fact she would be fine if we just made videos that she and I can watch together," Ravi said. I left out a sigh of relief. I pictured her sitting in the corner of his room fingering herself while we fucked and my cock deflated a little. It would be weird enough to see her around campus or with Ravi but to have her in the room was a step too far.

I know it seemed like a double standard because I would kill to have just about any guy stroke his cock in the corner watching us fuck but that too is also who I am. Another thing that worried me about this whole thing was Dave. He'd said he was also bisexual. What if he wanted to hook up with a girl? What if he wanted her to join us? I didn't know how I would handle that. It might test our relationship but I'd cross that bridge when or hopefully if we came to it.

"So any plans for the holiday?" Ravi asked.

"Yes, I've invited Dave to come home with me for Thanksgiving," I said.

"Oh nice!" Ravi said.

"I think I'm going to finally come out to the rest of my family," I said.

"Wow, that's a big step," Ravi said.

"I know, I'm worried, my mom is super conservative," I said.

"Yeah, you really need to think about it," he said.

"I have, I love Dave and he loves me. I don't want to hide it anymore," I said.

"Ok, just be prepared for the fallout. I know I'd be disowned if they ever found out about me," Ravi said.

"But now you have a girlfriend so the pressure is off," I said.

"I'll admit it does help relieve some of the pressure, but next it will be when are you getting married? Then, when are you having children? They hint at it every time we talk," He sighed.

"At least I don't have that kind of pressure," I said.

"Be grateful," Ravi said, so are we going to quit gabbing and make this video?"

"Huh?" I asked.

"Can you fuck me already and film it?" Ravi said getting up, pulling down his pants and getting into position on all fours on his bed. He held up his phone already switched to camera mode.

"If you insist," I said dropping my pants and pulling off my shirt. My dick was already semi hard and rising.

"You'll have to send me a copy as well," I said finding it a little awkward to hold the phone and get my cock lined up with his hairy ass.

I took a few establishing shots to show Ravi's body and his already hard and leaking cock. Then a close up of his ass winking at me, looking soft and ready to take me.

I pushed down my cock and slipped it into his warm hole trying to remember to aim the phone at the action while I sank into that beautiful hairy brown hole. I looked forward to showing it to Dave as much as Ravi wanted to show it to Amani.

It was definitely a turn on to watch myself fuck him through the camera angle like I was watching a porn and also staring in it. Maybe I should just quit school and make money streaming myself fucking and getting fucked? I had the dick for it? If engineering didn't pay off I'd have to consider it.

Ravi started moaning loudly, more so than usual. He typically tried to keep things quiet but I guess now he didn't care who knew how much he loved was getting railed by a big cock.

Suddenly he pulled himself off my cock and flipped over, his cock standing up and drooling all over his belly. He pulled his legs back and held them showing off his cock, balls and hairy taint. I scanned the phone up and down his body and got down and took his cock in my mouth. He grabbed the phone seeing that I was totally out of frame. He picked up filming from his perspective letting me focus on his cock. He grunted and moaned as I performed for the camera. I licked his balls then moved down his taint and licked around his ass.

"Oh fuck she is going to love this," he said holding the camera up to catch my tongue flicking at his hairy hole.

I stood back up and held up my cock to show how big and thick it was and then once again pressed it to his opening. He got a good shot of me entering him then shot a selfie of his expression as I fucked him. He held the phone in one hand and his cock in the other and stroked himself while I held his legs and fucked him hard.

What started out as somewhat over exaggerated moans and grunts turned into more realistic grunting and panting as he got into it. I was hitting his prostate hard and his cock was leaking all over his belly. He balls were tight against him and I knew he was close.

I wasn't too far behind him when he erupted all over his chest. He caught the lines of cum spraying his hairy chest.

"You want my nut in or out?" I asked frantically. I was at the point of no return. His fluttering ass was massaging a big load to a head.

"In, breed my hole good," he yelled.

"Oh fuck!" I cried as I filled his hole. He caught the moment I started to cum and the jerking of my cock and balls as I filled him with a creamy center. As I pulled out he caught my cum pouring from his used hole.

"Holy fuck that was hot," he said after he finally put down the phone and I had a chance to cuddle with him for a bit. I missed the more tender fucking we had done the previous time. This was the mechanics of sex without a lot of the emotion. Maybe that was for the best. His emotional attachment was for Amani just like mine was for Dave.

He sent me the edited video complete with transitions and fades like a professional porn video. Maybe he had a career in film editing if engineering didn't work out for him.

I'd show Dave later after his last game of the regular season. I had to get dressed to go watch.

## CHAPTER 27

# DAVE: QUARTERFINALS

The crowds roared, and I knew somewhere up in the stands was Brian watching me race toward the goal. I saw Todd charge to the right and kick the ball over to me. I slid into it, and the ball flew past the goalie into the net. The buzzer sounded, and the scoreboard lit up with the final score of the game: 2 - 1 in our favor. We'd won! I almost couldn't believe it. I felt my body being lifted off the ground by dozens of hands. I'd never felt anything like it. The adrenaline was coursing through my veins, my heart racing. They carried me off the field to join the throngs of fans spilling out of the stands to greet us.

"Great kick!" cried Coach as he grabbed me and lifted me off the ground as the rest of the team surged in around us, a mass of bodies flailing in exuberant glee.

"Fantastic game, everyone!" he called out as he hugged the rest of the team.

"We're in the finals!" Matty shouted with glee.

"I can't fucking believe it!" cried Bull, grabbing Tommy by the ass and hoisting him in the air so his crotch was nearly in his face as they spun around.

I saw him standing next to Ravi toward the back of the crowd, looking proudly at me but also looking a little lost.

I pushed my way toward him, flung my arms around him, lifting his skinny frame off the ground and into the air. He laughed as I spun him around.

"You did it! I guess you'll have to plan on a trip to the playoffs in December now," he said, smiling and sniffing back a tear of joy.

"I want you there with me! You're my lucky charm," I said, grabbing him by the back of the head and pulling him toward me. We kissed, and the crowd melted away. It was just the two of us basking in this glory together. He opened his eyes and glanced sideways at my teammates gathered around us. Some wore shocked expressions on their faces, while others smiled knowingly. I didn't care what they thought. I just knew I loved Brian and wanted to share this moment with him.

Bull looked over at Tommy and grabbed him by the waist. A gasp went up all around us as Bull, one of the most masculine straight-acting guys you'll ever meet, pulled Tommy in for a kiss. Not just a peck on the cheek but a full-on tongue wrestling wet snog. Brian and I beamed at them. Matty looked a little horrified but did not say anything, looking over at me sheepishly.

"Great match! Our teams back home would wipe you off the field, but it was adequate," Ravi said, giving me a wry smile.

"I know football here is light years behind the rest of the world," I said, hugging him and messing up his hair.

"Great shot!" Todd said, coming up and hugging both of us.

"Great assist! I wouldn't have made it without you," I said, pulling him close for a hug as well. Todd looked around nervously as I smacked his ass.

I spotted a man in a suit heading toward us, flanked by two tall, imposing-looking men. Each wore an earpiece and seemed to be continuously scanning the crowds. The man in the middle of the two mountains of muscle on either side of him was blond-haired and handsome for an older guy. He wore a suit with a flag pin on the lapel and hair that was either a toupee or surgically implanted on his head. Something about his face seemed familiar, but I couldn't place it. Clearly, he was someone important to have bodyguards with him.

"You must be David," he said, holding out his hand to greet me.

"Uh, yeah," I said, looking around to try to figure out how he knew me. My first thought was that maybe he was a friend of my uncle. He knew a lot of well-connected people for his job.

"This is my father," Todd said suddenly, stammering to say his name. He had the look of a small boy hiding in the shadow of his father.

"Nice to meet you," I said, though from what Todd had told me, it wasn't exactly nice to meet him.

"Good game," he said with a glint in his eye. I caught him scan down my body to my bulge and quickly look away. Did he just check me out?

"My son told me you are the team's star player and the son of a missionary," he said. Todd must have played up my background to make me appear more palatable to be hanging out with his son, rather than someone who was corrupting him.

Todd looked at me weakly, but I just smiled politely. I could see the type of man his father was, concerned primarily with image and the next campaign; other things like his son took a back seat to his ambition.

"Yes, you would really like my dad. I'm sure you have a lot in common," I said, thinking to myself, like molesting children.

"It's good to see Todd has found some good role models," he said.

"Yes, he's taught me a great deal, really improved my technique," Todd chimed in. I wondered what technique he was referring to. I wouldn't be starting my assistant coaching position until next season. I grinned at him thinking about how I'd taught him to suck my dick without using his teeth; he had definitely improved in that technique.

"Well, it was nice to meet you. I have to get going. We should have you up for dinner sometime," he said. I smiled politely, thinking that was as likely to happen as me returning to Africa to help with my father's ministry.

Brian stood by, fading into the background while Todd's dad was there, but as soon as he left, it looked like his head was about to explode.

"What is it?" I asked.

"I know him!" He said excitedly.

"Yeah, I think I've seen him on tv," I said rolling my eyes back in my head.

"No, a while back he sucked me off!" Brian burst out.

"What?" Todd and I both said, looking at him in disbelief.

"He cruised me in the library restrooms," he said.

"When?" Todd asked.

"Back in September. I was studying and needed a little relief, so I went into the bathroom. He was there at the urinal. I'm sure of it,"

Brian said. The library bathrooms were known to be a popular cruising spot on campus. It was almost guaranteed that if you were there, you were looking for dick.

"Fuck! He was here for a meeting of the board of trustees back in September," Todd said, looking in the direction his father and his security detail had gone in utter disbelief.

"I remember because I could feel those hair plugs he has when I was holding his head ..." Brian looked up at Todd, realizing he had majorly overshared. "Sorry."

"I can't fucking believe it," Todd spat.

"I can," I said.

"I told you, the most homophobic guys are almost always the biggest closet cases," Ravi chimed in.

Todd shook his head, his fists balled up in anger. Like he might try to chase after his father, overpower his security detail, and punch his lights out. As Matty could attest to, Todd was no slouch in a fight.

"Just relax," I said. "Now you have leverage over him."

Todd looked at me, puzzled. Then, like poison running through his veins, the ideas began to form in his mind, and a smile crept across his face.

"It is going to be one interesting Thanksgiving," he said, still looking into the direction his father had gone.

"Yes, it is," I said, mirroring his sentiments. I wondered what might be in store for us at Brian's house.

# DAVE: EPILOGUE

"Hurry up, it looks like a storm is coming," Brian said the minute I stepped through the door.

It was Thanksgiving Day, and I'd just come back from a friendly pickup game of football, American football that is, on the quad. It was a university tradition to play coed flag football on Thanksgiving among whomever was still on campus. Matty and Fischer were on my team. Todd and most of the rest of the team had already left for break. We won two to nil thanks to two awesome touchdowns by Fischer and me.

"Let me get changed," I said, setting down my gym bag. Brian was sitting on his bed, holding his backpack to his chest, and staring at the far wall.

"It's going to be okay," I said, sitting down next to him and reaching across his shoulder to hug him close. He'd been stressing for weeks about coming out to his mom.

"I want to tell them, but I'm scared," he said.

"You have every right to be nervous. You don't have to do it. I'm okay pretending to just be your roommate," I reassured him.

"No, I hate lying about it. I want them to know how much you mean to me," he said. I felt all warm and tingly inside and hugged him closer.

"I feel the same way. I'm just saying don't feel pressured to come out to them, especially now," I told him.

"Let's see how things go. I'll probably chicken out anyway," he said.

"See, that's the spirit," I said, giving him a friendly punch on the arm. He leaned in and got a whiff of my pits.

"You know I love your stinky pits, but you may want to shower and put on some deodorant before meeting your future mother-in-law," he asked.

"Mother-in-law? Is this how you are proposing?" I joked.

"No," he punched me back.

"I mean, I'm sure your dad wouldn't mind," I said. I'd not brought out what we'd done since it happened, and he looked at me a little shocked.

"I know he would," he said, giving me an evil grin.

"Jim is going to meet us there," I said, also hinting at possibilities.

"Well, don't just sit here. Go get a shower and get dressed," he said, smacking my ass.

"Yes, sir," I said, pulling my shirt over my head. I felt my shorts fall to the floor, and the room filled with my strong stench.

"I thought we had to get going," I said, looking down at Brian with his nose buried in my thick pubes, nuzzling the base of my growing cock. He cupped my balls and licked up my shaft. His dick was already hard and leaking.

"Just one for the road. We may not have a chance to do anything while we're at my house," he said. My dick was growing, pressing against his cheek as he looked up at me, batting his long eyelashes. I felt his tongue bathe my cock once more as it grew to its full size.

"How about a compromise? I get ready now, and you can blow me while I'm driving there," I said, tugging on my cock and slapping it on his tongue one last time.

"Deal!" He said, licking a bead of precum from my piss slit and taking another look, inhaling of my smelly balls before smacking my ass to get me going. I leaned down and kissed him, then turned and grabbed my towel and shower caddy.

This is going to be an interesting weekend, I thought, heading across the hall, buck naked. Most people had already left, so I didn't expect to run into anyone else. I was still hard, and while I'm okay walking to the shower naked, I tried not to offend anyone I might pass with my erection.

I was only a few paces out when I noticed a girl staring at me from down the hall. She'd just come up from the stairs. She smiled at me, then looked down at my dick. Her smile grew. I quickly put the towel in front of my hard dick and smiled at her sheepishly. She looked as if she was heading down the corridor toward Ravi's room, but she stopped and headed toward me instead. I felt like a trapped animal. I was in big trouble if she reported me. She should know what she might find coming onto a boy's floor unannounced.

"Are you Dave?" She asked, holding out her hand. I had my shower caddy in one hand and my towel in the other, but I juggled both while trying to retain some modesty.

"Uh, yeah," I said, taking her soft hand in mine.

"Ravi's friend?" She asked, looking like she wanted to be sure before she said anything more. Well, now she knew who I was, so she could positively identify me for public safety.

"I'm Amani, Ravi's girlfriend," she said, smiling shyly. It all clicked into place, and I let out the breath I had just now realized I was holding in.

"Oh, hi," I said in a much more friendly tone.

"Ravi's told me so much about you," she said. I blushed, knowing just how much he had told her. Brian had shown me the video he had sent to Ravi to send to her and told me how much she was into the fact that Ravi was bi.

Who would have ever imagined that behind that shy-looking, demure girl was the tiger that Brian had described to me? I blushed, thinking of the videos of us he'd also shared with Ravi. No doubt they had watched them together, talking dirty about all the things Ravi wanted to do to me and have me do to him.

"He's told us so much about you as well," I said.

She was hotter than I had expected, though again, I wasn't sure what I had expected. I certainly didn't expect a girl at all, given what he and Brian got up to.

"I just wanted to say hi. I'll let you go take your shower," she said, looking sadly at the towel that was hiding her view of my cock. I blushed even redder.

"It was nice to meet you," I said.

"Nice to meet you too. I hope we can all hang out together soon," she said, the undertone clear. I gulped. I think Ravi was itching to have me fuck him in front of her. I would definitely consider it. I'm just not sure how Brian would feel about it. Maybe after we get back from Thanksgiving break.

"Uh, yeah, we should," I said, trying not to commit to anything before talking it over with Brian. Though I still found girls attractive, I'd found I was becoming much more attracted to guys lately.

I left her to continue toward Ravi's room, and I continued into the shower room to get ready. We had a long drive and what could be a tumultuous weekend ahead. I hoped things went well meeting his mother, but I strongly suspected it would not.

As we walked to the student parking lot, I could see the clouds were moving in, and a cold wind was blowing. We got on the road heading off campus and then onto the highway.

I saw Brian grab his crotch out of the corner of my eye. He was clearly hard. I took one hand off the wheel and moved it to his thigh, letting my fingers move up it slowly toward his crotch. He smiled as I found the head of his dick trapped in his jeans. He looked out the window to see if there were any cars around and then popped the button. He hauled out his hard dick, letting it rest against the red sweater. I reached out and held it, feeling his hot skin in the frigid car. I cranked up the heat a little, then stroked him a few times, feeling him begin to leak down my fingers. I licked the precum off my fingers as he reached over to feel my hard dick through my jeans. He reached under the waistband and grasped it tightly. His hand was cold, and I jumped when it touched my thigh.

"Your hands are like ice!" I said, nearly swerving out of my lane.

"Sorry," he said, pulling his hand out of my jeans and holding it in front of the vent to warm it up.

"I know something that is already warm," I said, not taking my eyes off the road.

"I know just the thing," he said, taking my hint and leaning over toward me. He pulled my dick out once more, only this time I felt his warm mouth slide down my pole.

"Mmm, that feels good," I said, as his tongue got to work on my sensitive shaft.

HONK!, came the loud horn on my left. I nearly swerved off the road. I looked over to see a semi alongside us. There was a man in the passenger seat looking down at me with a grin on his face. He'd seen us, and the horn was his sign of approval. Brian looked up and spotted him as well. He held up my cock to show the trucker, then went back to work on it. Another blast of the horn came, but this time I was prepared for it. I leaned back in the seat to hopefully give him a good view. He was bearded and maybe in his mid-thirties. I pictured the driver looking similar, the typical bearish-looking truck driver type. I imagined them pulling out their hairy cocks and stroking them while they watched us, his buddy relaying all of the details to the driver.

I saw a sign for a rest stop a couple of miles up the road and was tempted to pull off and see if the truck might follow us in. I pictured both burly truck drivers taking turns fucking Brian while I watched and then fucked his used ass, lubed up with their cum.

"Oh, fuck," I cried as my load hit the back of Brian's throat. I couldn't take it anymore, knowing they were keeping pace with us to watch Brian go down on me, and the fantasy of them fucking him sent me over the edge.

Brian kept my load in his mouth, then opened wide, looking out the window at them with a mouth full of my cum. There was another loud honk and a thumbs up from the trucker before they passed us. The rest stop exit was already going by, and it was too late for either of us to stop. Brian kissed me, and I could taste my seed on his lips.

"That was a nice load," he said, licking his lips while he stroked his cock.

"Don't get any jizz on your nice sweater," I suggested. He pulled it up, exposing his bare midsection. I saw something white hit the windshield that was not his cum, then turned to see his balls tightened as his load coated his fuzzy abs.

"Here," I said, handing him a few napkins from the center console.

"Thanks, I needed that," he said, beaming at me.

"OK, put that away before we get pulled over," I said.

"I thought I'd just go in like this," he said, leaving his dick out while buttoning up his jeans.

"I bet you would too if it was just your dad," I said.

"I most definitely would," he said, tucking his dick away.

"Looks like it's starting to snow," I said, turning on the wipers.

"Hopefully, we'll make it there before it gets too bad," he said.

"I hope so too," I said, looking at the ominous clouds ahead.

# ABOUT THE AUTHOR

Kevin Davis, the author of steamy MM romance titles such as *The Quarterback and His Son, Helping Out My Straight Neighbors, Beast of Gaea, and Deep Fake*, is known for his ability to create complex characters with profound emotions and infuse his writing with intense passion and sensuality.

Davis's works transcend genre boundaries, delving into themes of love, loss, and the complexities of human relationships, all set against diverse settings that range from ordinary to the extraordinary.

He wrote short stories and his first novel at age 17 which led him to be accepted into the writing program at university. He took a break from writing to pursue a different career but continued to write and journal about his experiences.

He began writing erotic fiction based loosely on his journals and reminiscences for blogs and on Reddit. With the encouragement of his fans, he expanded these stories into full-length novels.

Contact the author at blueiguanapress@gmail.com

# ALSO BY KEVIN DAVIS

## THE QUARTERBACK AND HIS SON SERIES

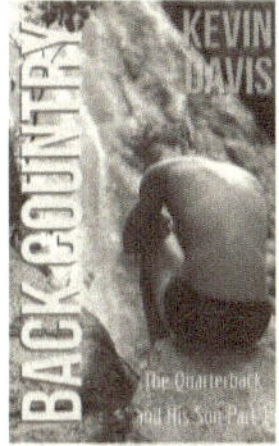

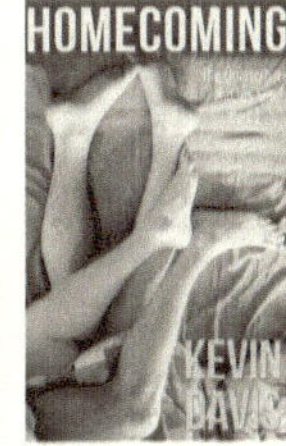

## OTHER WORKS

Coming
Soon

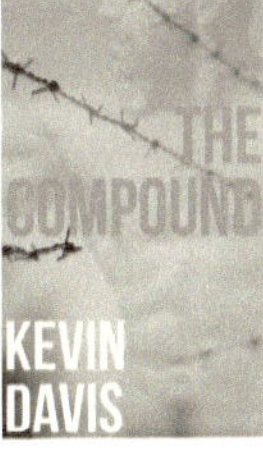

# Don't miss out!

Visit the website below and you can sign up to receive emails whenever Kevin Davis publishes a new book. There's no charge and no obligation.

## https://books2read.com/r/B-A-WAVX-TQXLC

Connecting independent readers to independent writers.